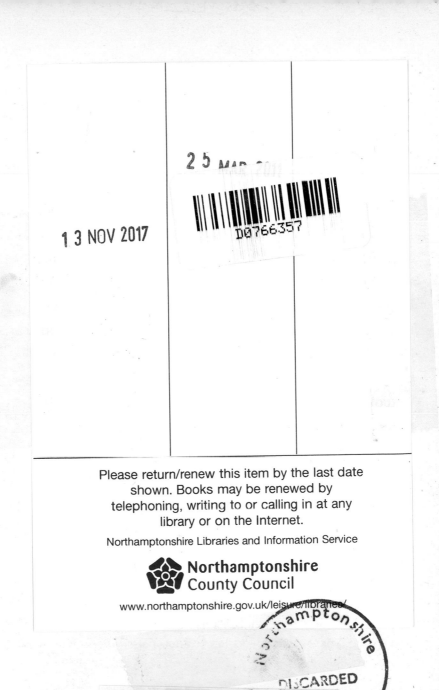

With thanks to Joe Winston, drama lecturer extraordinaire, and the fascinating women from my counselling course, without whom this book would not have been written.

First published in 2006 by Usborne Publishing Ltd., Usborne House, 83–85 Saffron Hill, London EC1N 8RT, England. www.usborne.com

This is a work of fiction. The characters, incidents and dialogues are products of the author's imagination and are not to be construed as real. Any resemblance to actual events or persons, living or dead, is entirely coincidental.

A CIP catalogue record for this book is available from the British Library.

JFMA JJASOND/06   ISBN 0 7460 7305 4   Printed in Great Britain.

# Meg Harper

USBORNE

# 1

Grace sat up with a soft cry. Something had woken her, she didn't know what. A sudden chill, a flutter on the air, the sound of a light footfall – it could have been any of these. She glanced around the room, lit up by bright moonlight. Grace left her curtains open at night; she hated the stifling feeling of having them closed even though they were as light and airy as she could persuade her father was decent. One of them fluttered in the breeze now.

*It must have been the wind,* thought Grace, snuggling back down under her quilt. But she wasn't quite satisfied. It had, she thought, been more of a smell – of wetness and brine, the cold damp air of the sea that her father brought into the house whenever he'd been fishing. She shivered, turned over and, just as her eyes were closing, noticed something odd. She sat up again, stared and then reached for the object that lay curled on her bedside table.

It was a necklace, delicately crafted from something that Grace couldn't place. Was it coral or mother of pearl? Were the polished beads, which glinted in the moonlight, made of some gemstone Grace had never seen before? She couldn't fathom how they had been strung together either. And they were so cold. It was a warm summer night but the gems in her hand held the chill of the ocean.

Grace smiled and rested the beads against her warm cheek, enjoying their cool, smooth touch against her skin. It must have been her dad that woke her then, sneaking in to leave this lovely surprise by her bed, a birthday surprise, for she would be fourteen in the morning. Odd, to leave a present there, unwrapped. But then her father *was* a bit odd; he had never seemed quite like anyone else's dad. Who else, after all, had a dad who was an artist?

Grace let the necklace fall gently back onto her bedside table. There was that smell again – damp and salty. It must come from the beads. She fell asleep with a smile on her face. The sea and her dad. Grace loved them both. The strange little beads were the perfect present.

"Dad?" Grace pushed open the kitchen door and was beaten back by the pall of smoke.

"Grace? What are you doing up? I was just going to bring you a birthday breakfast in bed!"

Grace laughed. "Forget it, Dad," she said. "You burning the toast woke me up. I thought the house was on fire."

"Sorry, love. I really ought to buy a toaster. I always forget about toast under the grill. This is my third attempt."

"Dad, you *know* why we haven't bought a toaster," said Grace. "Where would we put one?" She waved her hand around the tiny space that was their kitchen. Every surface was covered – dirty dishes, clean dishes, spice jars, a fruit bowl and a huge bread crock all jockeyed for space with heaps of books, papers and assorted pots of herbs. Every so often, Grace's grandma turned up and did what she called "sorting it all out". For a week afterwards, Grace and her dad would grouch around, unable to find anything, and then they'd have it back to how they liked it.

Grace took the plate of buttered toast that her dad was holding, cleared a space at the tiny table and sat down with it. Her dad passed her the jam.

"Happy birthday, Gracie," he said, giving her a hug. "Presents now or later?"

"Later," she said, laughing. "There's not enough time now. I'm going to have to hurry anyway or I'll miss the bus. I overslept."

"Did you?" said her dad. "I didn't notice."

"No, you're hopeless," said Grace. "In a world of your own."

"Sorry, love," said her father, his face falling. "I know I'm not a very good dad. Since your mum left..."

"Stop it, Dad!" said Grace, her voice unusually sharp. "Don't start the guilt trip. Mum left and that's that. I hardly even remember her. You're fine. I love you. At least you stayed."

"It wasn't her—"

"I said 'Stop it!', Dad. I mean it. It's my birthday – don't spoil it."

Her dad nodded. "Cup of tea, love?" he asked.

Grace gulped the hot tea he handed her and glanced at the clock. Had she time to ask him...? Yes, if she didn't, it would be on her mind all day.

"Dad?" she said. "You didn't leave me a present by my bed last night, did you?"

There was a sudden stillness in the room. Fleeting, barely there at all. But Grace noticed and her memory grabbed at it.

"A present? By your bed? No – all your presents are wrapped up and waiting for you in the studio. Why d'you ask?"

"Oh, nothing," said Grace. "It must have been a dream, that's all. But it was so vivid. I could have sworn it was real." She munched on her toast and watched her father's back. He was peeling carrots for her packed lunch. He tried so hard to be a good mum as well as a dad. Why on earth was she disappointed that she had dreamed the surprise beads? But they had been so lovely. She could almost feel the coolness of their smooth touch even now. They had seemed so real – the tangy, briny scent still seemed to linger in her nostrils. But it was no good – they weren't there now. She hadn't overslept; she had been searching her room.

"Never mind, Gracie," said her dad. "You've always had strange dreams – they've always seemed real to you."

"Yes, but this was even more real than usual," said Grace.

Her dad held out her packed lunch. "Well, don't let it

9

spoil your birthday," he said. "Just look forward to the presents you'll get tonight."

Grace nodded. "I'll have to dash," she said and crammed the last of the toast into her mouth. Five minutes later, she was running to the bus stop, worrying whether she'd stuffed the right books into her bag. But there was still one bright corner of her mind that said, "Necklace". The memory of those shimmering beads and her father's sudden, shocked stillness, sat patiently, waiting to be re-examined later.


"He's watching you again," hissed Jenna. "Don't look, but I'm sure he is."

"Don't be silly," laughed Grace. "Why would he bother to look at me?"

"Doh! Stupid question or what? He fancies you, idiot. It's obvious. Isn't it, Matt?" Jenna turned to Matt, who was staring out of the bus window.

"I wouldn't know about these things," said Matt. "Girls' talk, isn't it?"

"Hey, come on, Mr. Grumpy Gills! What's bitten you?" chided Jenna. "It's Grace's birthday! Lighten up!"

Matt pulled a face. "I was aware of that, actually," he said, "seeing as we've known each other since we were babies."

"Well, then..." said Jenna. "Don't be such a misery. What d'you reckon? Does Nik fancy Grace? Have you heard any rumours?"

"Look, Nik Bentley doesn't talk to the likes of me and neither do his mates," said Matt. "I might be a boy but I go to the local comp not the local posh school. I don't play rugby, I haven't got a state-of-the-art sailing dinghy or a dad on sixty grand or more a year. The only thing we've got in common is we get the same school bus. As far as Nik Bentley's concerned, I don't exist."

"And I don't either," said Grace. "Look, Jenna, he could go out with anyone he wanted to. He's hardly likely to hit on me."

"Then why does he keep staring at you?" said Jenna. "Don't tell me you haven't noticed!"

There was a silence. Grace pursed her lips, her huge brown eyes glinting with amusement. Matt held his breath. "We...e...ll," she said, her face breaking into a grin. "Well, okay then, I've noticed. But he's probably just thinking what a scruff-bag I look."

"There!" said Jenna, in triumph. "I told you so. Now all we need is some way of getting you two talking."

"Don't look at me," said Matt, promptly. "I've told you. I don't exist."

"Stop plotting, Jenna," said Grace. "He might look

gorgeous but he's probably horrible underneath."

"Or gay," muttered Matt.

"You wish," snapped Jenna. Their eyes locked angrily. Grace, however, had her head down in her bag.

"Oh no!" she said. "I've left my joggers at home. I knew I'd forget something!"

"Grace, you won't need joggers!" said Jenna. "It's going to be a gorgeous day. Just wear your shorts for PE. And sit up – quick! He's coming over!"

"His is the next stop," said Matt. "He's not coming over, he's getting off."

But Matt, to his disgust, was wrong.

Nik Bentley stopped by their seats.

"Hi," he said. "It's Jenna, isn't it? And...Grace?"

They nodded. Matt glared.

"I heard it was your birthday, Grace," said Nik. "Many happy returns. Are you doing something nice to celebrate?"

"Oh...err...just going out for a meal with my dad and my gran," said Grace, flushing scarlet. Jenna nudged her. "And Jenna's coming too," she added.

"And then we're going down to the beach for a swim," said Jenna. "You can come too, if you want." Grace gasped but Jenna ignored her.

Nik smiled. "That'd be great," he said. "What time?"

"About eight, I should think," said Jenna. "Thurle Bay. You can't miss us."

"Is that okay then, Grace?" asked Nik. "It's your birthday, after all. Mind if I muscle in?"

"Err...well...there'll only be me, Jenna and Matt," she stammered. "It's not exactly a party."

"No worries," said Nik. "Anyway, here's my stop. I'll see you later."

He and the other boys from the private school got off the bus. A few of them gathered round Nik, clearly joshing about what had just happened.

"You see?" crowed Jenna. "I told you so. He's been plotting this for weeks. He is seriously smitten, Grace, I'm telling you. You have pulled big time!"

Grace sighed. "I wish you hadn't asked him along tonight, Jenna," she said. "I don't even know the guy. Like I said, he might be horrible. And when he sees me in my swimsuit, he might completely change his mind about fancying me."

Jenna stared. "Why on earth would he do that?" she demanded. "You are seriously sexy, my girl."

Grace shrugged. "Let's just see how it goes, okay? You never know – it might be you that he's after, really."

\* \* \*

13

Considering she spent it at school, Grace had quite a good birthday. Several of her friends had brought presents and she had double art in the afternoon, one of her favourite lessons. She skived rounders, pretending she had a headache and lay in the shade reading. The only blot on the landscape was an unpleasant interchange with Mr. Thomson, the Head of PE.

"You've missed our training swims for two weeks running, Grace," he said, catching her in the corridor at lunchtime. "What's going on? We're relying on you for the next schools' gala but I can hardly keep your place in the team if you don't come to training."

Grace flushed. "I swim in the sea nearly every day, Mr. Thomson," she said. "I'm twice as fit as anyone else in the team. You can rely on me, honestly."

"That's not the point," he retorted. "You've got to show commitment. The other kids need to see that. I know you're good but I can't make you a special case. If I let you skip training, there'll be others at it and what am I supposed to say to them?"

Grace stared at the floor. That was his problem, wasn't it? Why drag her into it?

"Grace, I want to see you at training without fail from now on," he said. "Otherwise, I'll have to consider dropping you."

"Drop me then," muttered Grace.

"What was that?"

Grace raised her head and met the teacher's anxious eyes. "I hate swimming pools," she said. "You know that. I hate the smell and the feel of the chlorine. I've swum loads for the school and got you loads of medals and I still can – but I don't want to come to training any more. In fact, I'm *not* coming to training any more. You can't make me. I'll swim in the sea and I'll still be the best you've got. Take it or leave it!"

"Grace Hornby!" gasped the PE teacher, shocked rigid. "What on earth has got into you?" Grace, with her huge, sensitive, brown eyes and her gentle manner, was the last kid he'd expect to turn on him like that.

But she had gone, running off down the corridor with all the grace of her name. "Stop running!" Mr. Thomson yelled after her, in frustration. Then, muttering under his breath, he stomped off to find her form tutor.


Grace ran to the toilets. There, she locked herself in, sat on the loo and sobbed as quietly as she could. She hated disappointing Mr. Thomson; he was a nice man and he didn't deserve it. But she couldn't go to training any more. In fact, she couldn't see how she was going to manage galas any more, despite what she'd said. Which reminded her. Nik would be at the beach later. What on earth was she going to do about that? Honestly, sometimes she could strangle Jenna! Her and her big mouth!

All in all, it wasn't until she was toiling up the hill to the cottage that Grace remembered her dream. Matt was by her side. Jenna lived in the village but Matt's home was a B&B in the lane that finished at Grace's cottage.

"Matt, I had another of those dreams last night," she said.

"The birthday dreams?"

"Yes – but this one was *so* real."

Matt shrugged. "You always say that."

Grace smiled. "I know – but, honestly, this time I could smell the sea and I can still feel how the necklace was cold against my cheek."

"So it was a necklace this time?"

"Yes, and Matt, it was soooo beautiful!"

"More beautiful than the shell-backed mirror?"

"Yes."

"And the mother-of-pearl comb?"

"Yes. Do you remember them all?"

Matt shook his head. "No – not all of them – but they seem to have got more beautiful every year."

"They can't go on for ever," reasoned Grace. "My imagination will run out of ideas. When d'you suppose they'll stop?"

"Dunno. I'm not a dream expert. Maybe if you ever find out what happened to your mum?"

"Yeh, that's what they're about, I suppose, even though I always think the presents are from Dad. I guess I'm just wishing that she'd show she remembered me – just once a year, just a little bit."

"Not just a little bit," said Matt. "Those presents are very special. Unique. Maybe you're actually a mermaid in disguise. It'd fit, wouldn't it? Great swimmer, dreams about gifts made of shell and coral, gorgeous long blonde hair. Dead obvious, really."

Grace grinned. "Don't you think my hair should be more exotic? Sea green or turquoise perhaps?"

"Seems exotic enough to me," said Matt.

"You can talk! What about yours?"

Matt shook back his mop of striking red hair and laughed. "Pity it's my best feature," he said. "Great hair, shame about the face."

"Oh, come on, Matt," said Grace. "You're not exactly..."

"Nik Bentley?"

Grace hit him playfully. "I was going to say 'ugly', idiot! Anyway, Mr. Thomson used to keep going on at me to have my hair cut. Reckoned it'd make me faster."

"I'd have killed him if you had," said Matt.

"Well, I decided it made no difference. I still beat everyone else, most of the time. So he left me alone. He's not going to leave me alone now though – not now I've told him I won't train in the pool."

Matt looked puzzled. "You're serious about that, aren't you? What's that all about then?"

Grace flushed, kicking herself for having mentioned it. "Oh girls' stuff. Don't worry about it. Just a few problems with...well...you know..."

"Oh, okay, forget it," said Matt, looking uncomfortable.

They walked on in silence for a few paces. Then, partly to cover the awkwardness, Grace blurted out, "I asked my dad this time."

"What?"

"I asked my dad about the present. Whether he'd left it for me."

"Really? What did he say?"

"That he hadn't, of course. That I'd always had vivid dreams – well, I do, not just the birthday dreams. But he seemed...well...I don't know...I don't know how to describe it. It was only for a moment...but he seemed stunned."

"Well, it must have seemed a bit odd," said Matt. "I mean, if he had left the necklace for you, why would he have taken it away again?"

"No reason. He wouldn't, of course. I was stupid to ask. But, I don't know...there was just something about him. Something that made me think he knew about the necklace. It was weird."

"Grace, careful!" said Matt. "You're letting this get to you. You're *wanting* the necklace to be real. It isn't. You know it isn't. You've been having these dreams for years and there are never any real presents. It's really sad but that's the way it is."

"I guess you're right," said Grace, sighing. "You must be right. There isn't any other explanation."

They stopped at Matt's gate and he fished around in his schoolbag.

"Look, I haven't given you my present yet," he said and pulled out a small parcel.

"Ooh, can I open it now?" asked Grace.

"Of course."

Grace unwrapped the paper and unfolded the tissue inside. There, in her hand, lay a tiny, mother-of-pearl-backed handbag mirror.

"Oh, Matt!" she gasped. "It's beautiful!"

"The best that *Accessorize* could provide," he said.

"Specially manufactured by Merpeople for Merpeople."

"Idiot!" laughed Grace, tucking away the mirror carefully. "It's lovely, though. Thank you so much. I'll see you later then, okay?"

Matt looked unhappy. "Actually, Grace, is it okay if I don't come down to the beach tonight?" he said.

"What? Why not?"

"Loads of homework. Sorry, I've let it mount up. Stupid, I know."

Grace glared at him. "That's rubbish, Matt. If you're going to lie, you'll have to do better than that. You just don't like Nik Bentley because he's too posh. Well, be like that, if you must – but I'd rather you came, all right?"

With that, Grace turned on her heel and stomped off up the lane.

"It's not because he's too posh," muttered Matt, under his breath.

# 2

"Well, are we allowed to give you your presents now?" asked Grace's dad, reaching out and stroking her cheek lightly with one finger.

Grace grinned. "Oh, I guess so," she said. "I just never like it all to be over. That's why I keep putting it off." That was true enough: her dad didn't need to know that the last shred of wrapping paper always ended that year's hope; the hope that her mum might, for once, have sent her something.

She, her dad, her gran and Jenna were sitting waiting for their desserts in the renowned seafood restaurant in the village. They didn't eat there often; a bistro with quite so many rosettes, stars and recommendations didn't come cheap. But Gran liked to treat them for birthdays now that Grace was old enough to appreciate it. Grace was allowed to invite one friend and, of course, it had to be Jenna. She would have been devastated if Grace had asked Matt.

The presents were predictable. Grace was never sure what she wanted and always ended up with a heap of girl stuff – bath potions and make-up, CDs and books, pretty fripperies of every sort. She appeared to revel in it all without discrimination. But today there was something special.

"Grandma!" she cried, her soft brown eyes alight. "This is perfect – it's exactly what I need – but you shouldn't have! It must have cost the earth."

"Well, I saw people using them in the Olympics and I thought you might like one," said her grandmother, a touch tight-lipped with embarrassment at Grace's delight. She wasn't the sort of grandma who gushed. "I know *I* wouldn't want to swim in the sea in a skimpy little cozzie – and they're supposed to make you faster too, of course."

Grace held up the present for the others to see. It was a gleaming lycra bodysuit, the sort Ian "Thorpedo"

Thorpe had made famous. It was deep, deep green but as it caught the candlelight, it glowed with iridescent pinks and purples, like leaked petrol.

"Wow!" said Jenna. "You'll look fantastic in that, Grace! Figure-hugging or what?"

"That's not why I bought it," said Gran, looking severe. "I thought it would be practical."

"Oh, it will be," Grace assured her. "Very practical indeed. In fact, I can try it out tonight at the beach."

"What?" said her grandmother. "You're not thinking of going down to the beach this evening, are you?"

"Well, not right now," agreed Grace. "But a bit later. When we've recovered from this fantastic meal. We're meeting a couple of friends. We'll have a swim, make a fire and roast some marshmallows. Nothing dodgy, Gran, honestly."

"Robert, did you know about this?" Gran demanded.

"Uh...well, yes, of course I did," said Grace's dad. "Grace often goes for a swim in the evening. I don't see a problem. It'll hardly even be dark tonight."

"So who are these friends you're going with?" persisted Gran.

"Just Matt and this guy who gets the school bus with us. He's called Nik Bentley."

"Never heard of him," said Gran. "Is he from the village?"

"Yes, but the other end. Somewhere along the road to town."

"Hmm...the overpriced new-build then. Not a local, is he?"

"Gran!" Grace rolled her eyes. "It doesn't mean he's an alien, you know, even if he has only lived here a few years. He's just a boy, same as Matt, and you don't mind him."

"I've known Matthew and his parents since they were babies. You know where you are with locals. You know what you're up against."

"Mum, let's just leave it, shall we?" said Grace's dad mildly, though Grace could see from the flush that had risen around his collar that he was annoyed. Grace's mum hadn't been local. She'd come from "just along the coast". As far as Gran was concerned, that meant she might as well have been a goblin.

"Mrs. Hornby, we're only going for a swim and a bit of a campfire," put in Jenna. "It's not like we're planning an orgy!"

"What did you say, young lady?" said Gran. "An orgy! I should think not indeed! Dear me, where do you young people pick up these words? I didn't even know what sexual intercourse was at your age!"

It was unfortunate but at that very moment the

restaurant went quiet. Several people turned to look at Gran in surprise. Jenna and Grace nearly exploded with giggles but catching the look on Grace's dad's face, managed not to.

"Ah," announced Gran, staging a haughty recovery. "At long last! The desserts!"

In relieved silence, the girls tucked into their puddings. *Let's just hope,* thought Grace, *that Gran's dessert will take her mind off Nik Bentley. Not that I really want to see him tonight but I'm going to feel a real idiot if we're not allowed to go.*

Later, outside the restaurant, when Gran was safely stowed in the front seat of the car, Grace's dad spoke to the girls.

"I'm going to run your gran home, Gracie. You two can walk back and get this beach trip sorted out. That way you won't have to put up with any more nagging."

"But *you* will, Dad," said Grace.

"I can handle it," he grinned. "I'm a big boy now."

"Will you come down and join us later?" asked Grace. "You can if you want."

"Wouldn't you rather be on your own with your friends?" asked her dad, surprised.

Grace shrugged. "Doesn't matter. Like Jenna said, we're not exactly planning an orgy."

"Well, maybe I will pop down," said her dad. "I haven't swum for ages and it's a beautiful evening."

"See you later then," said Grace and swung off down the road.

Jenna ran to catch up. "What on earth did you want to ask him for?" she demanded. "What if you and Nik want to...you know..."

"Want to what?" asked Grace. "Snog? Make out? Have an orgy? Wouldn't that make you and Matt feel just a little bit left out?"

"It wouldn't matter," argued Jenna. "We wouldn't mind."

"Well, it's not going to happen, okay? I've barely met him. I don't even know if I like him yet. And if you can invite *him* down to the beach on my birthday, then I think I can ask my dad, all right?"

"Oh, all right. But won't Nik think it's a bit odd if your dad comes tagging along?"

"So? If he does, then he's an idiot. There's nothing wrong with my dad. Nik ought to be honoured to meet such a respected artist; lots of people would die for the chance."

"Yeah, I know that," said Jenna, frowning with frustration. "I just meant that he's probably not used to girls having their dads tagging along on a date, no matter how 'respected' they are. It's not exactly cool, is it?"

Grace laughed. "Jenna, when will you get it into your thick head that this is *not* a date? You just invited Nik down to the beach, that's all."

"I bet *he* thinks it's a date," said Jenna, grumpily. "I bet he's expecting a bit more than swimming and toasting marshmallows. Honestly, Grace, you and your dad, you need to catch up with the twenty-first century. Sometimes I wonder if you've come from a different planet!"

"Jenna, we're just different, that's all," said Grace. "Why's that a problem? It'd be awful if everyone was the same."

Jenna grimaced. "I suppose," she said. "I just think that if you've invited a guy who fancies you down to the beach, you ought to make a bit of an effort to be more normal. Like not take your dad with you. And at least kiss him goodnight."

Grace stiffened. "Jenna," she said, her voice very level but very firm. "You are beginning to really annoy me. *You* invited Nik down to the beach, not me. I'm sorry if I don't fit into your photo-love story but that's the way it is. If *you* want to snog a complete stranger then get on with it – I won't stand in your way. All right?"

There was an awkward pause. Then Grace slipped her

arm through Jenna's and squeezed it. She rarely got cross and hoped she hadn't said too much.

"Come on," she said. "It's my birthday. We shouldn't be arguing. I'll race you up to the cottage, okay?"

Matt was already waiting when they got to the cottage. He was sprawled on his back on the scrubby grass that surrounded it. He sat up as they approached.

"I thought you weren't coming," said Grace. "Too much homework, wasn't it?"

"Yeah, well, I finished quicker than I thought," said Matt. "You took your time though. We'd better hurry before it starts getting chilly."

"Sorry," said Grace. "We had to walk back because Dad decided to drive Gran home straight away. She was getting stressy about us going down to the beach."

"Don't tell me," said Matt. "*Young people nowadays – we never did that sort of thing in my day!*"

The girls smiled at his impression.

"Exactly," said Grace. "And as for going with a boy who wasn't born in the village – well, anything might happen! We'll probably all come back pregnant!"

"Including me?" laughed Matt.

"Especially you," said Grace. "Who knows where Nik

comes from really? He's probably an alien!"

"Well, the alien might give up and fly off in his spaceship if we don't hurry up," said Jenna. "Come on, let's go and change."

In the bedroom, Grace unravelled her lustrous bodysuit.

"Just going to the loo," she told Jenna and hurried out.

Once safely in the bathroom, she stripped off her clothes quickly. She stood for a moment, peering at herself closely in the mirrored doors on the cabinet. Then she pulled the little switch that lit them up. It was no good. There was no mistaking it now in that bright, revealing light. She couldn't pretend any longer that she didn't have a problem.

She had known for a long time all about the bodily changes that happen when you're a teenager because her dad had taken care to explain. Her first period had been no surprise about nine months ago and she was happy with her neat, firm breasts – not too big and not too small – well, so far, at any rate. She hardly had any trouble with spots – maybe the sea water helped with those – and hair had appeared in all the right places. It was the hair in the wrong places that worried her.

She knew that lots of girls shaved their legs and

around their bikini line too. Living by the sea, they spent a lot of time in shorts and swimsuits on the beach. They shaved whenever they showered as a matter of course. That was all normal. It was something else that was happening to her.

Grace examined her shoulders more carefully. No, she had never seen anything like it on anyone. This was fine, close-growing fair hair and it covered her – her back, her arms, her stomach, her legs – everywhere except her hands, her feet and her face. Thank heaven for that, at least. Grace shuddered at the thought of it spreading there too. She ran her hand down her leg. The hair was soft, short as velvet, like she imagined a mole might feel. Because it was so fair, she had barely noticed it when it had begun to grow, a few months back. It was possible that no one else would notice it either. But Grace didn't think so. It was thicker now and, when she was cold, it stood on end. It didn't make her ugly; she knew that. But it did make her odd. Weird, as Jenna would say. And Grace, whatever she might bravely say, didn't want to be *that* weird. Her obsession with swimming marked her out as it was.

At first she had waited, terrified, to see if it would grow longer. It didn't. It stayed as it was, barely three millimetres long. She often thought about shaving it off but she knew, from the other girls, that once you started shaving, your hair tended to grow thicker and quicker. She couldn't take that risk – and anyway, how could she shave her *back*? Or her breasts? The very thought made her shudder. She wondered if it was something hormonal and if she ought to see a doctor but that might mean telling her dad and, much as she loved him, she couldn't bring herself to do it. A furry daughter. Grace almost gagged. How could her dad ignore the truth – that his only daughter was a freak? He'd reassure her, of course.

"You're beautiful as you are," he'd say, pretending nothing had changed. "Who cares what other people think?"

Well, Grace did. She couldn't help caring what everyone would think – including her dad. She knew she was pretty and, though she'd never really bothered about boys till recently, she'd always felt a pleased sort of glow when she'd received valentines. And she was flattered that Nik Bentley, who was in Year Eleven, was interested in her, even if she didn't know if she liked him yet. But what would he think if he knew she was covered in fur? Because that was what it was. Very fine, very short, very blonde – but fur, nonetheless.

Wracked with worry, Grace got into the bodysuit. She was supple and could reach the zip at the back easily. She smiled bravely at herself in the mirror and pulled on her joggers and a thin sweatshirt. Her fur was hidden for now. What she would have done if Gran hadn't given her the bodysuit, she didn't know – claimed she was cold and worn her wetsuit, perhaps.

"Grace? Grace? What are you doing in there?" called Jenna. "Are you okay?"

"Oh, just admiring my lovely bodysuit in the mirror," Grace replied, forcing a laugh into her voice. "Sorry – d'you need the loo?"

"No, I just think we should hurry."

Grace opened the door. "Come on then," she said. "Let's go and wow Nik Bentley."

# 3

Robert Hornby walked slowly down to Thurle Bay. It wasn't the main beach for the village because it wasn't perfectly sandy, and along the waterline there were concealed rocky patches which got in the way of a smooth dash in or out of the water. Nonetheless, it was a safe bathing beach and it lay just beneath his cottage. He and Grace knew it intimately; the rocky shoreline was no bar to their swimming or fishing. He wondered, as he strolled down the steep path, whether this Nik Bentley had even known it was there. Probably not, he thought. These young incomers liked "facilities": burger vans, chilled fizzy drinks on tap, surfboard hire and flush loos. Not for them the simple pleasures of swimming and fishing.

He gave himself a mental shake. What was he thinking of? He was just as bad as his mother! How dare he, of all people, make assumptions about people who weren't local? How dare he pigeon-hole them and make them fit his own picture of the world? Hadn't he learned his lesson long ago? This Nik Bentley was a unique person, just as he was himself. Just as Grace's mother had been.

*This Nik Bentley.* Robert couldn't stop thinking of him like that. How many others did he know of? None. So why "this" Nik Bentley? Why the suspicion that immediately went with his name? He knew the answer, of course. "This" Nik Bentley was the one who was interested in "his" beautiful daughter.

Robert wondered if he was biased. Did all fathers feel like this – that their daughters were the most beautiful in the world? He had tried to look at her objectively; he was an artist, after all, trained to spot the truly lovely. He hardly ever got further than her face, so reminiscent of her mother's. It was rounder than it should be if she were a conventional beauty, with a wide, gently curving mouth.

It was framed with thick, straight blonde hair that hung to her shoulders. She had plump, rosy cheeks and a smattering of freckles across her slightly snub nose. All that was nothing more than pretty. It was her eyes that made him weep with longing for the wife he had lost. Deep, dark, fathomless brown, huge and set wide apart, as if to allow space for the dense, long eyelashes which made them appear bigger than ever.

And now he wasn't the only male of the species to have noticed. Unconsciously, Robert clenched his fists. If this Nik Bentley hurt his little girl, he would kill him!

No. Robert laughed at himself. He was a gentle, kind, tolerant man. He had learned to be. People had to choose their own paths; forcing your own will upon them only led to pain. If Grace and this boy went out together, who was he to complain? They had their own lives to live. And after all, Grace was only just fourteen. She had plenty of time to choose. What was he panicking for? Really, he was a joke. He seriously needed to sort out his brain.

Robert paused where the cliff jutted out and stood on the mini-headland, staring out into the bay. There they were, the four of them. The blond boy – that must be Nik Bentley. No, he wasn't as at home in the water as the others, you could see that from here. But why should he be? Robert watched them, an indulgent smile on his face as they dived and leaped, showing off to each other. Like young seals. Or dolphins.

He started down the last stretch of path and then hesitated. Did Grace really want him here? Had she just been humouring him, her old dad, not liking to leave him out on her birthday? Why would she want him around her young friends? Perhaps it would be better to say he had felt tired, that he had needed an early night? Yes, he would duck out – leave Grace to choose her own path without the pain of watching.

But then she was waving at him and he could not ignore her. She was emerging from the sea, mermaid-like in that glistening green bodysuit that made it all too obvious that she was no longer a little girl.

"Dad!" she yelled. "Dad!" Then she yelled something else but she was too far away for him to hear.

"I'm coming, Gracie!" he shouted back and started jogging towards her.


Grace's dad stayed until the last marshmallow had been toasted.

"Well, I'm off now," he said. "I've got an early start – I want to drive along the coast to catch the dawn light. There's a good weather forecast so I'm hoping to be lucky."

"Is it only landscapes that you paint, Mr. Hornby?" asked Nik.

"Mostly," smiled Grace's dad. "That's what you'll see in the galleries round here. That's our bread and butter. Stuff for the tourists."

"That makes them sound awful!" said Grace. "And they're not. They're fantastic. They just glow with colour – and they...oh, I don't know...they don't just show a picture, they show feelings!"

"I know," said Nik. "I've seen them. We have three at home, actually. My mum and dad really admire your work, Mr. Hornby."

Grace gasped and even Grace's dad seemed taken aback.

"Wow!" he said, with an embarrassed laugh. "Looks like your mum and dad probably paid for the marshmallows then."

"Not really," said Nik. "But I did bring some bananas and chocolate flakes for us to roast."

"Great!" said Jenna. "That sounds yummy. What do we do?"

The awkward moment had passed and while they were all busy slitting open bananas, cramming them with chocolate and wrapping them in foil, Grace's dad slipped away. Grace almost called him back, suddenly frightened of what might lie ahead. Nik seemed nice. A bit of a wimp in the water, she thought, but that was hardly surprising – not everyone learned to swim before they could walk. There were other things about him that she liked – the way he had joined in with their games, the way he had persisted in being friendly to Matt even though he was at his grumpy worst, his politeness to her dad. And she couldn't help but notice that his body matched up to the handsomeness of his face. He sailed, he told them, and he played rugby for his school; that kept him pretty fit. Grace and Matt could outstrip him easily when they raced in the water, but Jenna had to make an effort to hold him off. Grace didn't want to admit it to herself and certainly not to Jenna after the fuss she had made, but the thought of Nik suddenly *pulling her to his manly chest and seeking her lips in the darkness* – yes, the sort of sloppy stuff that Jenna was always reading – made her tingle with excitement. And terror.

After the bananas, squidgy, sticky and burning hot, they worked hard to clean up their mess. It was dark now but the moon was bright and they could see well enough to make several trips to the water's edge with an old bucket, to fetch water to wash away the embers.

"How are you getting home, Nik?" asked Grace, expecting that his mum or dad would pick him up.

"Oh, I'll walk," he said. "It's not far. That's how I got here. No worries."

"But you can't walk along the beach to the village now," said Jenna. "The tide's in. You'll have to come with us up the path to Grace's cottage. It'll take ages."

Nik shrugged. "Never mind. It'll keep me fit."

Grace looked worried. "My dad would give you a lift but he'll have gone to bed," she said. "I'm sure he wouldn't want you to walk all that way at this time of night. There's no pavement once you're out of the village. It's quite dangerous really. Can't you give your mum or dad a ring?"

"Well, yes, of course I can. I just..."

"Wanted to look macho," muttered Matt, so only Grace could hear.

"...didn't realize about the tide. Sorry. Stupid really."

"Oh no," said Jenna. "Why should you? We only know because we've lived here for ever."

"Well, phone them then," said Grace. "Dad'd be really cross if he found out you'd walked. Come on, we'd better get going."

Grace strode ahead and the others followed.

"Here, Grace," said Jenna, catching up with her. "I'll take the bucket and the rubbish. You shouldn't be carrying all that on your birthday. Matt – be a gent – carry Grace's towel for her!"

"Don't be silly, Jenna," said Grace. "I'm fine."

"Don't you want to hold Nik's hand, idiot?" hissed Jenna. "You seem to be getting on very well!"

Grace handed Jenna the bucket but hung on to the towel and slung it round her neck. "Happy now?" she said.

Jenna shook her head. "I wonder what the time is?" she announced loudly. "I hope it's not too late."

Nik rooted in his pocket for his mobile. "Just gone ten," he said.

"Oh no!" gasped Jenna. "I'm late! Matt, come on, we'll have to hurry or I'll get in terrible trouble."

"Don't be silly, Jenna!" said Matt. "You never get in terrible trouble."

"Oh, I will," said Jenna. "Mum's gone terribly strict. I didn't do too well in my SATs, remember? And I said you'd walk me back. Come *on*, Matt – hurry!"

Matt hesitated. "You sure you'll be all right, Grace?" he said.

"Matt, I go up and down this path all the time," said Grace. "I'll be fine. You sound just like my gran."

Matt turned his back and stomped after Jenna.

"Sorry," Grace said, turning to Nik. "I don't know what's got into him. He's really moody these days."

"Probably fancies you," said Nik. "Doesn't like me being around."

Grace stared. "What? Matt? Don't be stupid! We've known each other since we were babies!"

"So? That wouldn't stop me. You're gorgeous, Grace."

He glanced up the path, then took her hand. Gently, he pulled her towards him, slung off the towel from her neck and slipped his arms round her waist.

*Oh no, it's happening,* Grace panicked. *He's going to kiss me!*

And then he did and she stopped panicking and concentrated on kissing him back.

Later, Grace couldn't sleep. The excitement of her first kiss had fired her adrenalin. She relived it again and again. The touch of Nik's fingers seemed to have burned itself into her back. Her brain was in a whirl. Did she really like him? Should she have let him kiss her? She had agreed to meet him again soon – but did she really want to? Her life had been calm and simple for so long. She barely remembered her mother ever having been there, she had left when Grace was so small. It had been just her dad, the sea and herself, the steady routine of school, Matt, Jenna and swimming – for years. She was never bored. If she was restless, the beach and the sea had always soothed her.

And now this. She had never been so fired up, not even before a big gala. Every nerve, every muscle, every brain cell felt on edge – and just because a boy had kissed her. She couldn't describe the strange sensation that had slid through her body when his hand had touched hers – a jolt, a shock, a surge – but intensely exciting. The nearest she could get to it was the feeling of diving into the sea on a clear, cold morning when every pore seemed burst open by the chill. But that sensation wore off quickly. This had gone on and on whilst he kissed her until she had thought she would explode.

She got out of bed. It was hopeless; she would never sleep feeling like this. Her bodysuit was wet but that didn't matter. It was well past midnight. There would be no one to see her. She slipped off her nightie and pulled on a swimsuit, joggers and a sweater. Moments later, she was on the path to the beach. She had left a note on the table:

*Gone for a midnight swim. Love, G*

She didn't expect anything to go wrong but she left it, just in case.

The contrast a couple of hours made was amazing. Grace was used to the beach at night but had never been there alone so late. There was a stillness and quiet about it that surprised her. Surely it couldn't be so different? Surely it was all in her head? Nonetheless, it was thrilling. It was as if a whole new beach was beckoning her which, at the same time, was an old friend too.

Grace stripped off her jersey, joggers and sandals, ran gleefully through the shallows and dived into the waves. Bliss! She had never understood why other people stood at the edge shivering, testing the water with their toes before gradually easing themselves deeper into the water. Even Matt and Jenna did it sometimes on windy days. She couldn't wait to hurl herself into the surf, impatient for that startling, zinging touch which made her feel twice as alive.

Grace swam hard, a strong, powerful front crawl taking her swiftly a good kilometre out to sea. It was a calm night and her body rose and fell with the gentle waves as easily as a dolphin. Then she paused, lay on her back and floated, bobbing gently, water lapping over her face as she gazed up at the moon. She felt rested, peaceful, as comfortable as if she was in her bed at home; it would be easy to fall asleep here. But she knew that she mustn't. She must set off back for the bay at once. Much as she loved the sea and felt at home in it, she didn't underrate its danger. The gentle rise and fall of the waves could lull her to her death. She understood very well where stories of mermaids and sirens had come from.

She swam back, a slow, leisurely breaststroke now, savouring each moment that her face ducked beneath the surface and the dark water was lit eerily by the moon. She only wore goggles in swimming pools, where the chlorine made her eyes red and sore. In the sea, she was as comfortable as on the land. Understandably, she thought; tears, after all, are salty.

She was just short of the bay when she saw them, their streaming heads gleaming in the moonlight. They were in their usual place, swimming and basking on the rocks at the end of the headland that divided Thurle Bay from the rest of the coastline. A colony of seals. Could they see her, she wondered? They never seemed alarmed by her presence, never swimming away or raising their voices. Sometime they even came up quite close, peering at her with their great doe-eyes. She supposed they were used to her; they had been sharing this bay since she had first been able to swim to the end of the headland and maybe before. She had the dimmest of memories of clinging to her mother's back as she swam out this way, hanging onto her thick plait of brown hair and crowing with delight. But perhaps that had been a dream; something she wanted to have happened but which never had.

Tonight a trio of seals broke away from the group and swam closer to her, following her at a distance until she was well into the bay. Then they fell back and she swam on alone.

Back on the beach, she rubbed herself down briskly, delighting in the glow she felt from head to foot. She pulled on her clothes and yawned. Yes, she would sleep now. All that tingling, disturbing energy had gone. It would be an effort to climb the path but the thought of snuggling down into her bed again spurred her on. She ran across the beach and started up the track.

She was halfway up when she suddenly froze. She had heard something; something that shouldn't be there. A rustle or a crunch or a pebble skittering back down the path. She glanced behind her. No, there was no one there. How could there be? She was tired and probably half asleep, almost in her dreamland where all things seemed so real. But she didn't feel half asleep; she felt wide awake suddenly. Every nerve seemed alert to the possibility that there was someone or something behind her on the path; something watching her, following her. She began to run. She must get home quickly. She was too tired, it had been too exciting a day – her imagination was playing tricks on her.

She reached the top of the path, panting, and stopped

to stare back the way she had come. Silly! There was no one there, of course there wasn't, and now she had made herself hoarse with effort. She took a few deep breaths. The night was silent and still, but for the heaving of the sea. It felt normal. Empty.

Grace crept into the cottage and crumpled the note for her dad. Moments later, she was fast asleep under her quilt, as if felled.

# 4

"Matt, have you ever walked in your sleep?" Grace asked the next morning, as they strolled down to the bus stop together.

"Don't think so. Why?"

Grace gave an inward sigh of relief. She had wondered if Matt would be as surly as he had been down at the bay but he seemed his usual self.

"It's just I had this really strange experience last night. I was walking back from the beach..."

"What? With Nik? Or was this part of a dream?"

"No." Suddenly, Grace wondered if she should have started telling Matt. Did she want him to know that she had kissed Nik? She could see Matt asking far too many questions. "I went back again later," she continued, fast-forwarding.

"On your own?" Matt sounded shocked.

"Yes. Why not? I couldn't sleep. It was a lovely night. What's the problem?"

"Grace, anything could have happened! And no one would have known!"

"I left a note for my dad – just in case – but, Matt, what could have happened? I'm a brilliant swimmer."

Matt shuddered. "I don't know, I just don't like the idea of you down there in the dark on your own."

"Matt, you sound like my gran again! What d'you think happens down there at night? D'you think gangs of druggies hang out or smugglers send in boats? D'you think mermaids are going to kidnap me? Honestly, there was no one there but the seals and me. It was fantastic."

To her surprise, Matt took her arm in a strong grip. "Grace, don't go there at night on your own. Please. You really shouldn't. If you're that desperate for a midnight swim, come and wake me up. Please. Promise me."

Grace shook him off. "No, Matt. Don't be silly. I'm not promising you anything. You're being a real old woman."

Matt kicked at a pebble angrily. "Have it your own way, then," he said. "But don't blame me if something goes wrong. Anyway, you were saying. About walking up from the beach."

Grace felt so cross that she almost couldn't carry on. What had got into Matt? He'd been grumpy most of yesterday and now he was turning into a control freak! Maybe it was a boy thing. Raging hormones making him all overprotective or something.

"Well? Aren't you going to tell me? The suspense is killing me."

"Sorry," said Grace, pulling herself together. "Sorry to be so ratty. I'm probably overtired."

"Yeah, you probably are – messing about in the sea in the small hours – serves you right! Why couldn't you sleep anyway? I was knackered when I got in."

"You had to walk Jenna home," Grace pointed out, carefully avoiding the question.

"What time did Nik go then?"

"Oh, his mum arrived just after we got back," said Grace.

"Kiss him goodnight then, did you?"

"Nosy!"

"Bet you did. Bet that's why you couldn't sleep. I'm right, aren't I?"

Grace flushed furiously. "What's it to you if I did? There isn't a law against it! Anyway, I was telling you about when I was walking back later..."

"Go on then. I'm not stopping you."

He *was* stopping her; his whole grumpy body language was seriously off-putting. But Grace was desperate to tell someone. She ploughed on.

"The thing is," she explained, "that I suddenly felt sure someone was following me. I heard something – I don't know what – and then it just felt like someone was there."

Matt stopped. "Where were you?" he asked.

"About halfway up the path."

"You didn't see anyone then?"

"No. No one. It was just a sound and then a feeling. And the sound could have been anything – some little creature crossing the path. It was the feeling that seemed so real. So I just wondered if I might have fallen asleep for a moment but kept walking – you know how vivid my dreams are. D'you think that's possible?"

Matt nodded slowly. "Yeah, I don't see why not," he said. "You might not have been properly asleep, just very dozy."

"So you don't think there was anyone there really?"

"What a druggie or a smuggler, you mean? A mermaid would struggle to get up the path with her tail."

"Don't tease, Matt. You *know* what I mean."

Matt shrugged. "Why are you asking *me*? I've just told you that you shouldn't go down to the beach at night because you never know who might be there. You say that's stupid. But now you're telling me you think someone followed you! What d'you *want* me to say?"

"Oh, I don't know," said Grace, her face screwed up with anxiety. "It just worries me that I have these dreams that are so real. I thought maybe this was another one. No one else seems to have them. They make me feel so weird! Like I'm not normal."

"Well, *I* don't think you're weird," said Matt. "And Nik doesn't either, by the sound of things. Well, weird enough to want to kiss him, of course, but he didn't seem to mind that."

"*He* kissed me!" protested Grace. "I didn't start it! And before you ask, that's all he did, okay?"

"Hey, slow down," said Matt, with a grin. "Too much information! Anyway, if someone was following you, at least they didn't catch you. And if it *was* a dream, it won't kill you. But like I said, I wouldn't go down there alone at night, okay?"

They were almost at the bus stop and Jenna ran to meet them.

"Well?" she demanded. "Well? Did he kiss you? Did he try anything else? Are you going out? When are you seeing him again?"

Grace pushed her away. "Shut *up*, Jenna," she said. "How can you say things like that? Put it in the local paper, why don't you? I'll tell you later, okay? Look, the bus is coming."

Grace hid her blushes under her hair as she rummaged for her bus pass but Jenna's words had struck chill into her heart. How many dates could she expect to get through before Nik *did* try something more intimate than kissing? She shuddered. What on earth was she going to do? Never go out with him again? That shouldn't be a problem. She'd been perfectly happy before she'd met him; she could be perfectly happy again. But then she remembered how she'd felt when he'd kissed her. Was she never going to feel that way again? Was she never going to go out with boys, never get married, never have children, just because she was the world's one and only girl who happened to be covered in fur? It just wasn't fair. She was going to have to do something about it.

\* \* \*

"Mr. Hornby?"

"Speaking."

"Mr. Hornby, it's Andy Thomson from school. Grace's PE teacher."

"Really? What can I do for you?" Robert couldn't keep the surprise out of his voice. "There isn't something wrong is there?" He virtually never had phone calls from the school. Grace was calm and organized and easy-going, never getting into arguments, never forgetting kit or homework and only ever late if there was a problem with the bus.

"Well, I'm not sure if there's anything wrong or not," said Mr. Thomson. "I was hoping you might be able to help me with that."

"What? Is something wrong with Grace?" Robert demanded, panicking. "I'll come immediately if there is."

"No, no, it's nothing like that. I'm sorry, I shouldn't have alarmed you. It's just that she hasn't been coming to training the last few weeks and...well, you know how much we rely on her. She's our star swimmer. But I can't let her stay on the team if she doesn't come to the training. It wouldn't be fair on the others."

Robert was flabbergasted. Grace always seemed so open and honest, he sometimes wondered how she would get on in the world. Would a little less transparency be a good thing? Now, faced with this deception, he was thunderstruck. Well, maybe deception was a strong word. She'd never actually said she was going to training when she wasn't; he'd never asked. She always dealt with her swimming kit herself and he'd just assumed she was going.

"Mr. Hornby?" said Mr. Thomson. "Are you still there?"

Robert came to with a jerk. "Yes, yes, I'm still here, I'm just amazed, that's all."

"Oh...er...right...she hasn't mentioned anything at home, then?"

"No, not at all. She's been just the same as usual – swims in the sea most days, whatever the weather. Of course, she's always been sensitive to chlorine and occasionally that's put her off swimming at school – you know, if it's been particularly strong one day – but I can't remember the last time that happened."

"So she hasn't lost interest in swimming then?"

"No, certainly not. Unless when she says she's going swimming, she doesn't. I suppose that's possible. But it seems so unlike Grace." Robert was clutching at straws. Grace always returned with wet kit and smelling of the sea. And she'd been so thrilled with that bodysuit the day before. She *couldn't* have taken against swimming.

"Well, maybe you could check that out, Mr. Hornby?"

suggested Mr. Thomson. "I want to get to the bottom of this. Kids change such at lot at Grace's age. They do give up swimming – especially the girls. All sorts of worries about body changes and messing up their hair – it's depressing even though I'm used to it. But somehow, I never thought it'd happen to Grace. She's always loved swimming so much – almost like stopping swimming would mean stopping breathing."

"Yes, yes, I know," said Robert. "It's only to be expected."

"What? That she'd lose interest, you mean? Like she's done so much she's got sick of it? I do hope not."

"No," said Robert, floundering. "I didn't mean that at all. I was just...well, I'm sorry...I was just thinking about what her mother was like. She loved swimming..." He stopped to clear his throat. "But she left, you know. When Grace was small."

"Yes, Mr. Hornby, I'd heard. I appreciate it might be difficult for you to tackle the subject with Grace – if it's one of those girl things. Perhaps you have a female friend who could...? Or is there a teacher Grace particularly likes?"

Robert quickly scanned the women he knew. His mother? Good grief, no! Jenna's mum? Or Matt's? No, they were both nice women but he knew Grace would be hurt if he asked one of them to tackle a potentially delicate subject. He had told her the facts of life himself, for goodness' sake! Surely he could ask her why she was skipping training!

"It's all right, Mr. Thomson," said Robert. "Leave it with me. I'll do some investigating and get back to you as soon as possible."

"Thank you, Mr. Hornby. I'd be very grateful. It's not just that we've got a big gala coming up, it's that I'm a bit concerned about Grace. She's been quite rude about it – very unlike her. It could just be puberty kicking in but maybe there's something specific troubling her."

"Thank you, Mr. Thomson. I appreciate your concern," said Robert. "I'll see what I can do."

Robert put the phone down and sat back on his haunches. He felt completely unsettled. As planned, he'd worked for a couple of hours in the early morning light and had come home in time to see Grace off for school. She'd looked tired but that was only to be expected after quite a late night out with her friends. He hadn't been worried; it was only a day and then it would be the weekend. Now, however, he was questioning her every move. He stood up and wandered through to the cubbyhole that they called the utility room. The light on the washing machine showed that it had finished its cycle. Robert unloaded it, looking for clues. One of his few conflicts with Grace was over washing swimsuits and towels. He thought she washed both far too often.

"You could just rinse out your costumes and hang up your towels to dry. They'd last much longer and it'd be more environmentally friendly," he'd say.

Grace would ignore him. "They smell too fishy," she'd argue. "I don't mind but other people might."

Sure enough, the brand new bodysuit was there in the heap, along with two swimsuits and three sports towels. *Thank goodness that Grace didn't mind using tiny microfibre towels*, thought Robert. *Without them the washing machine would be on non-stop.* Whenever he swam in the sea, he liked a good thick terry towel to wrap up in afterwards but Grace hardly seemed to feel the cold and would rub herself down with a sports towel, sling on a few clothes and race back to the cottage for a shower.

Surely Grace wouldn't wash her kit if she *hadn't* been swimming? Even if she was trying to deceive him, he couldn't imagine Grace thinking of that. But then he had never imagined her mother would do anything behind his back – until she did.

A great wave of grief rose up and threatened to engulf Robert. He shut his eyes and gritted his teeth. His hands clenched the damp swimsuit that he held. He would conquer this; one day he would conquer this, he told himself as a sob rose relentlessly in his throat. Not today though. He slumped down beside the pile of wet washing and let the tears pour down his cheeks.

Later, Robert set out along the cliff path. He had done every bit of housework he considered needed doing, forced himself to eat lunch and swallow a huge mug of camomile tea and still he couldn't settle to paint. A walk, he decided, would do him good. He had to get himself together before Grace came home; he had, after all, to try and find out what was going on. It was a lovely, early-June day, warm but not hot and with a light breeze blowing off the sea. He was a lucky chap to be able to enjoy it. Many a man would be stuck in a hot, sweaty office and be facing a long commute home in heavy traffic. He would stop feeling sorry for himself and count his blessings instead. Grace had been an easy child; he could hardly complain if the worst problem he had to face was her skiving swimming training!

An hour or so later, calmed but hot and sticky, he was retracing his steps. Thurle Bay lay before him, deserted and enticing. The sand stretched out below him, smooth and welcoming. From this distance, he couldn't see the patches of rock and shingle. The sea, shimmering in the afternoon sun, was a deep, Mediterranean turquoise. Robert felt an irresistible urge to do something he hadn't done for years – to strip off his clothes and take a spur of the moment dip. If he hurried, he could still be back in time for Grace.

He hurried down the path, dumped his clothes on a rocky outcrop and, in just his boxers, ran into the sea. The shock of cold didn't thrill him as it would have done Grace but he felt refreshed the moment his body hit the water. He struck out strongly across the bay and then flipped over to relax on his back and let the waves rock him for a while.

It was then that he noticed the seals. He should have expected them to be there, of course, basking in the late afternoon sun. In his rush of enthusiasm, he had forgotten them. They saw him and began to honk in alarm.

*Damn*, thought Robert. He wasn't frightened of them, of course he wasn't, but they didn't like him. He avoided disturbing them if he could. Slowly, trying to move in a way that suggested no threat, he swam back to the shore.

He ran back up the beach, shaking himself more or less dry. Then he scrambled out of his boxers and pulled on his clothes. He paused for a moment to look out to sea.

Were the seals still watching him? They hadn't left their rocks and seemed happy enough. But Robert's calm had been shaken. As he stared out at them, imagining their huge, sad eyes, again he had to fight a tide of misery and longing.

Slowly, he started to climb the path.

Grace could see that her dad was on edge about something. He was fidgeting about the kitchen, straightening piles, watering plants that didn't need watering, wiping and re-wiping the surfaces.

"Dad, what's the matter?" she said, at last. "You're making me nervous. How can I get on with my homework with you twitching about all over the place?"

Grace always did her homework in the midst of the cluttered kitchen table. She liked to be near her dad and he, having worked alone for hours, enjoyed her company while he cleared the dishes, cleaned his brushes and sorted things out for the next day. Often, he would join her at the table to do some paperwork or would simply sit and read. They had no sitting room as such; Robert had taken that over to turn into his studio. There was a sofa and a tiny TV in the corner but the kitchen was a much more cosy place to be.

Robert sat down at the table now.

"Grace, I'm sorry," he said. "I was trying to wait until you'd finished. There's something I have to talk to you about."

Grace raised an eyebrow. Had Mr. Thomson contacted her dad – or was she about to get a pep talk about the dangers of going out with boys? She hoped it was the former.

"Grace, Mr. Thomson rang today..."

Grace breathed a sigh of relief and for possibly the first time in her life, thanked God for her grandma. Two days ago, Grace didn't know how she would have answered her dad's questions. Now that she had her bodysuit she could lie. Though she didn't like doing it.

"Oh, it's okay, Dad," she said. "I know it's stupid but I guess it's my age. I just began to feel funny about the boys looking at me...you know what I mean?"

Her dad nodded. Yes, he could imagine that the boys might stare at her; he certainly would have done at that age.

"To be honest, Dad, I wasn't sure what I was going to do. I was too embarrassed to tell Mr. Thomson. And then Gran went and got me that bodysuit. It's brilliant – I don't know why I didn't think of it myself."

Her dad looked dubious. "They might still stare,

Gracie," he said. "I'm sure you'll still look very...how can I put it? Very..."

"Sexy? Well, maybe – but at least I won't feel so *naked* – as if their eyes are just boring into me all the time."

It was her dad's turn to breathe a sigh of relief. So that was all it was. Phew! Simple!

"So I can tell Mr. Thomson you'll be going back to training, can I?" he said.

"Oh, don't worry," said Grace. "I'll tell him myself on Monday."

Her dad put his arms round her and hugged her hard, his lips nuzzling her hair. "I'm so glad that's all it is," he said. "I was so worried when Mr. Thomson phoned."

"Dad!" said Grace. "You are silly! I bet you got yourself all worked up. I hope it didn't stop you painting."

Her dad said nothing for a moment; he wasn't going to admit just how worked up he had been.

"Grace, if there's anything else troubling you," he said. "Anything at all – you will tell me, won't you? I know how hard it must be, not having a mum around to talk about things but I'd do my best – whatever it was."

Grace buried her head in her homework. "I'm fine, Dad. Just fine. Stop worrying about me, okay?"

But he couldn't, of course.

And neither, if she was honest, could she.

# 5

"Mind if I come round to your house for a bit, Jenna?"
Grace asked, at the point where the road divided.
"There's something I want to ask you about."

"Fine," said Jenna, flattered. Even though Jenna thought
of Grace as her best friend, she always felt a slight distance
between them. Grace didn't give much away; if there were
any secrets Jenna suspected they were only shared with
Matt. Or maybe it was Nik these days. He and Grace had
been "an item" for a couple of weeks now. Jenna

sometimes wondered if Grace trusted boys more because of her mother leaving all those years ago; it would make sense. Jenna's mum had often talked about Mrs. Hornby's departure. It had been sudden. One day she was there and everything had seemed fine; the next day she was gone.

"And she's never been back to visit," Jenna's mother always added in shocked tones. "Not even once. How could a mother do that? Leave her little girl like that and never come back to see her? Of course, she always did seem a bit odd. Very pretty – like a dark version of Grace – but very cool. Very aloof."

Jenna had looked up aloof in the dictionary. "Away, apart, distant," it said. Like mother, like daughter then. Grace was friendly enough but it was always as if there was a separate part of her that was hidden from Jenna. It was a surprise then to have her wanting to ask about something – something that she clearly couldn't share with Matt.

Matt, meanwhile, had raised his eyebrows. "Oh-hoh," he said. "Girls' talk, hey? I know when I'm not wanted."

Grace gave him a light-hearted shove. "Yes, clear off, little boy," she said. "This is far too sophisticated for you."

Grace was silent as they walked along the road. Jenna realized that her jaunty dismissal of Matt had been a brave act. Whatever was on her mind, was serious. She could hardly bear the suspense. Was Grace having trouble with Nik? She knew from other girls how pushy boys could be. Or was it something to do with her swimming? She'd overheard some girls bitching about Grace because she hadn't been turning up for training. What was that about? Jenna knew Grace didn't like swimming pools as much as the sea but she'd never missed training before.

Jenna's mum was gushing in her welcome. As far as she was concerned, Grace was a poor, motherless girl. Oh, Robert Hornby did his best, poor man, but a girl needed a mother – especially at her age!

Jenna dismissed her mum's efforts quite rudely, in Grace's opinion.

"No thanks, we don't want a scone, do we, Grace?" she said. "Just leave us alone for a bit, can't you? We want to talk."

"But these are fresh from the oven!" protested Jenna's mum. "Come on, Grace! Have a cup of tea and a scone, love. I'm sure your dad never gets round to doing any baking."

Grace smiled politely. "May I have one later, please?" she said, backing out of the room after Jenna. "I'm not that hungry now."

"Humph! You girls!" said Jenna's mum. "Anybody'd think you were anorexic the way you carry on!"

"Ignore her," hissed Jenna, hurrying Grace up the stairs. "She's an interfering old bat!"

Grace winced. She got on so well with her dad that she couldn't quite understand it when Matt and Jenna were rude about their parents. But at least that meant she could rely on Jenna not saying anything to her mum about what she was about to tell her.

As soon as they reached her bedroom, Jenna closed the door with a flourish.

"Well?" she demanded. "What's the problem?"

Grace sat down on Jenna's bed. Now that the moment had come, she was having second thoughts. What if Jenna was disgusted? What if she thought it was so terrible that she simply had to tell her mum?

"Err...the thing is," she stammered. She glanced up into Jenna's curious eyes. Was she really the right person to tell? Well, there was no one else; what choice did she have? "Well, the thing is...there's something happening to my body that I don't think is normal. Well, I know it isn't normal, actually."

Jenna assumed an air of superiority. It wasn't often that Grace knew less than she did.

"You'd be surprised," she said. "Girls' bodies change a lot at our age. Bigger boobs, of course, bigger hips, periods, stomach cramps, hairy armpits..."

"Yes, I know," interrupted Grace. "Obviously. It isn't any of that. It's something else. I just wondered if you knew about anything that wasn't that obvious. Anything that's rare – but still normal."

Jenna looked stumped. "I don't think I do," she said. "Not off the top of my head. Some girls get really heavy periods, of course. And bad headaches. And some girls get really hairy legs so they have to start waxing them – even when they're only ten or eleven."

"Do they?" said Grace. "What? Just their legs?"

"Well, their arms as well, I think, and well...you know..." Jenna paused and blushed. "Around their bikini line too."

"Nowhere else?" Grace persisted.

"Gosh, I don't know, Grace!" Jenna looked uncomfortable. "Is that what the problem is? Have your legs got really hairy? Is that why you haven't been going to swimming training?"

"Who told you about that?" demanded Grace.

"Just some silly cows who were moaning that old Tommo would probably let you in the team anyway, even though you'd been skiving. They didn't tell me; I heard them going on."

Grace sighed. "Well, they can shut up," she said. "Now that I've got my bodysuit, I don't mind going."

"Is that what's worrying you then, Grace?" persisted Jenna. "Hairy legs? You don't have to cover them up, you know. Just get them waxed. There's a place in the village you can go. Lots of girls do."

"It's not that simple," said Grace.

Jenna nodded sympathetically. "You'd have to tell your dad, I suppose," she said. "It's quite expensive."

Grace shrugged impatiently. "It's not that," she said. "It's something worse."

"What?" asked Jenna. "You're not...you're not pregnant, are you?"

"What?" said Grace. "What on earth made you say that? We were talking about hairy legs!"

Jenna bit her lip. "Oh, I don't know! I just can't imagine what's worrying you so much. For goodness' sake, hurry up and tell me!"

For reply, Grace rolled up her sleeve. "Look," she said.

Jenna stared at Grace's arm. "What?" she said. "I can't see anything."

"Come closer," said Grace. "Feel it."

Jenna jumped off the windowsill where she had been perched and approached Grace. She reached out her hand tentatively. Deliberately feeling Grace's arm felt slightly uncomfortable.

"It's okay, Jenna," said Grace. "It's not what you're

thinking. I'm going out with Nik, remember?"

Jenna looked embarrassed. "Sorry, Grace. Sorry. It's just that...well, this is so weird."

"It'll get weirder in a minute. Hurry up, can't you? Look..." Losing patience, Grace grabbed Jenna's hand and plonked it on her wrist.

"God!" said Jenna, peering closely. "What is it? It's like...it's like velvet...or f-fur!" She clapped her hand over her mouth. "Oh Grace, I'm so sorry! That sounds terrible! Like I'm calling you an animal or something."

Grace looked grim. "That's how I feel," she said.

Jenna's eyes were round. "Is it...is it...just on your arms?"

Grace shook her head. Tears stood in her eyes, making them even more doe-like than usual. "It's...it's...all over me," she whispered, beginning to cry. "Except my face and hands and feet. I'm a freak, Jenna. They should put me in a zoo!"

Jenna flung her arms round Grace. Grace was always so calm. She couldn't remember ever seeing her cry. "No, don't say that!" she said. "It must be some hormonal blip or something! Look, we can go to the doctor. There's bound to be something they can do. Tablets or something. You've probably got too much hair-making hormone or something!"

"But it isn't like ordinary hair!" sobbed Grace. "It's too soft. It's like moleskin or something."

"Everyone's hair is different," Jenna insisted. "Some people's is really coarse, some people's is really silky. You know that!"

"The thing is," said Grace, scrabbling up her sleeve for a tissue, "I wasn't that worried – I thought maybe I'd grow out of it, or something – but now I'm going out with Nik and what if he finds out? I've only kissed him so far but...well..."

"I see what you mean," said Jenna. "I hadn't thought of that."

"I think about it all the time," said Grace. "I mean, even if I dumped Nik, what about other boys? Am I never going to get past kissing?"

"Nik may not mind," said Jenna. "You never know."

"But it's all over me," Grace wailed. "And it's growing thicker on my back! How can he not mind? And anyway, it's a pain covering up all the time. I want to wear shorts and strap-tops not trousers and shirts – it's the summer!"

Jenna looked cross. "It shouldn't matter, should it?" she said. "Not if Nik really loves you! Men are hairy and *we* don't make a fuss!"

"Not even men are hairy all over," said Grace.

"Some are," retorted Jenna. "I've seen them on the

beach. And they certainly used to be. Maybe it's some kind of throwback thing."

"That doesn't help," Grace sobbed. "That would mean I'm stuck with it."

Jenna paced up and down her room. Whatever she'd thought Grace was going to say, it certainly wasn't this. Really she thought Grace ought to tell her dad but obviously she didn't want to or she'd have done it already. Jenna thought about how she'd feel herself. She'd rather die than have to tell her mum she was covered in fur. But she couldn't think what else might help. She sat down on the bed beside her friend.

"Grace, don't you think you should tell your dad?" she said.

Grace shook her head furiously. "I can't bear to," she said. "I can't bear the thought of him knowing that I'm a...that I'm a freak. He's always been so proud of me. Everything about me. He loves me so much – I know he does – and I love him. I don't want to spoil it!"

Grace began to cry again and Jenna patted her shoulder helplessly.

"He would love you anyway," she said.

Grace shook her head. "No," she said. "I can't tell him."

Jenna took a deep breath. "In that case," she said. "I think you should go to the doctor. Your dad wouldn't have to know. There may be nothing they can do – but there might be. Do you want me to come with you?"

Grace nodded. "Yes, please," she said. "I've never been on my own before. I don't even know how to make an appointment."

Jenna smiled. "That's the easy bit," she said. "Now come on. Wash your face and let's go and have a scone. I could really do with one now – and a cup of tea with loads of sugar! Then we'll phone."


They were lucky. Jenna managed to get an appointment for after school. The doctor was a man but they'd discussed that before Jenna phoned. A woman would be preferable but Grace wanted to see someone as quickly as possible; telling Jenna had brought her misery to the surface. It seemed unbearable now.

Grace told her dad that she had extra swimming training and would get a later bus home. She felt dreadful about lying to her dad, especially when he smiled delightedly.

"So you feel a lot happier about it now?" he said. "Good old Gran – for once!"

"Yeah," she said, failing to meet his eyes. "Good old Gran."

Grace told Matt that she needed to buy a few things in the village. That was normal. He didn't bat an eyelid. Then she and Jenna hurried down to the surgery.

"I hope we don't meet anyone we know," said Grace.

"Silly!" said Jenna. "We're bound to. But don't worry. I'll do the talking."

Jenna was right. It was a large village but there were a good half-dozen people in the waiting room whom Grace recognized. One of them was Mrs. Potts, a retired teacher from their infant school. She seemed harmless enough. She was so busy asking them about how they were getting on at school that the reason they were seeing a doctor didn't arise until the last minute.

"One of you poorly then?" Mrs. Potts asked at last.

"Sort of," said Jenna, looking shy.

Mrs. Potts nodded sagely. "I know what it's like," she said. "They try to kid you that it's a real privilege, becoming a woman. But really it's a pain – that's why they used to call it 'the curse'. Ooh, I used to have the most terrible cramps myself..."

At that moment, a doctor popped his head round a door and called Grace's name.

"Well, bye then," said Mrs. Potts. "Lovely to catch up with you. I hope he manages to sort you out, love. Aspirin and a hot-water bottle, that's my advice. There's nothing to beat the old remedies."

The doctor was young and handsome.

"You didn't tell me he was drop-dead gorgeous," Grace hissed at Jenna as she gathered up her things.

"I didn't know!" muttered Jenna. "Sorry."

Grace gritted her teeth. If she died of embarrassment, at least that would be the end of her troubles.

"Take a seat," said the doctor. It was so long since Grace had been to the doctor that she couldn't think what to do. She sat nervously on a chair next to Jenna and waited.

"So which one's Grace?" asked the doctor, smiling.

"Me." "She is." The girls answered at the same time.

"So what can I do for you, Grace?" the doctor directed his smile at her – warm, encouraging.

"Err..." Now that the moment had come, Grace couldn't think how to start. If she said something about being too hairy, would he think she was just some silly teenage girl with a vanity problem? Desperately, she nudged Jenna for help but all she got was a quick, panicky glance.

"It's something very difficult to talk about?" said the doctor.

They both nodded.

"Something you can't talk to your parents about?"

They nodded again.

"Okay, well...can I ask the obvious question?"

"If you mean, is she pregnant, no, she isn't," Jenna blurted out.

"You're sure?"

"Yes!" said Grace.

Speaking broke the spell. Grace had begun to wonder if her tongue would remain clamped to the top of her mouth for the rest of her life. She pulled up her school shirt.

"Look at my back," she said, flushing scarlet. "I'm like that everywhere."

The doctor stood up and came over to examine her. If she'd expected a cry of horror, she didn't get one.

"Come here where the light's better," he said. She felt his fingers touching her lightly. Then he let her shirt drop.

"May I look at the front?" he asked.

"It's not so thick there," she said, pulling up her top again.

"I see. And you say it's all over?"

"Not my face and hands and feet. Everywhere else. Really. Everywhere."

"I understand. And apart from this, would you describe your body changes as normal for your age?"

Grace nodded. "I've got normal hair in the right

places," she said. "And my periods and everything. Do you know what it is? Is it a hormonal thing? Will it go away?"

The doctor indicated that she should sit down. He remained standing himself, twiddling with a pen he'd picked up.

"To be honest with you, Grace, I don't know," he said. "I've never seen anything quite like it before. I think we must refer you to a specialist – two, actually. One who specializes in hormonal problems and one whose area is dermatology."

"What's that?" asked Grace.

"I'm sorry – skin problems."

Grace gave a great sigh. "You think they might be able to help?"

"I hope so," said the doctor. "I'm afraid there's nothing I can do myself. The trouble is, there may be a long wait. Your condition isn't life-threatening so it could be several months before you're seen."

"Months?" Grace's voice was sharp with shock. "I can't wait months. What if it gets worse?"

The doctor's face was sympathetic. "You might be seen earlier if you went privately," he said.

"You mean she'd have to pay?" said Jenna.

"Yes."

"But then I'd have to tell Dad," said Grace.

"I know," said the doctor. "It's difficult. But think about it – it might be best to tell your dad. You shouldn't be embarrassed."

"But I *am* embarrassed," said Grace. "I can't bear it. He'll think I'm a freak!"

"Don't rush," said the doctor. "Take your time to consider what I've said. I'll refer you today and we'll just have to see what happens. You may be lucky. You may be seen really quickly; I'll make it clear that this is seriously upsetting you."

Grace stood up. There was no point in staying. The doctor had done all he could.

"Thank you," she said, forcing herself to smile. He had, after all, been very kind and tactful. He hadn't even asked awkward questions about her mum.

And then he blundered. "Try not to worry about it, Grace," he said. "Apart from this, you're fit and healthy."

"Exactly," she said, her voice suddenly quivering with fury. "*Apart* from this. *Together* with this, I'm just a freak!"

The doctor sprang into apology but it was too late. Grace stormed out of the room.

"Thanks," said Jenna nervously, picking up Grace's bag. "You've been really helpful."

"No, he hasn't," said Grace, as soon as the door was closed. "I feel even more like a freak now."

# 6

It was Saturday afternoon. Nik had phoned every day and Grace had enjoyed chatting but had carefully avoided being alone with him since she had seen the doctor on Tuesday. She "hadn't felt very well", she "had loads of homework", she'd "already planned to do something with Jenna"... But now she had a date with him that evening; she couldn't put him off any longer. In any case, she didn't want to. She liked him and she was missing the excitement of being with him. She saw him on the bus, of course, and they would sit hand in hand or with their arms wrapped around each other, but that wasn't enough any more. Grace would lie in bed, fantasizing about lying in his arms on the beach, but in her fantasies, her skin was smooth and golden. She would get as far as Nik gently beginning to lift her T-shirt and the dream would rip into a thousand hairy shreds. She would reassure herself that Nik wouldn't mind if she held him off; after all, in her father's youth, nice girls had never allowed boys "to go too far" as he put it. But how long would Nik put up with that? Even the most restrained boy might start to get frustrated after a few months. What would he do then? Call her frigid and chuck her? She'd known that happen to girls who didn't want to move as fast as their boyfriends did. And then there were her own feelings to consider too. It was awful to feel that she daren't let him touch so much as her bare arm. And it was getting increasingly difficult. She had told him that she always wore long sleeves because her skin was very sensitive to the sun but that was no excuse for not letting him touch her. What if she *did* let him? If he didn't mind, fine. But what if he did? And worse, what if he told other boys about her? It didn't bear thinking about.

"Don't worry so much," said Jenna as they walked up from the beach together. "You've not been together that long. It's not like you've been keeping him at arm's length for months already."

"I know, I know," sighed Grace. "It's just...well, it's going to be a beautiful evening and we're going for a walk and a swim and I just know that one thing'll lead to another and then..."

"Maybe you should do something different?" suggested Jenna. "I mean, you've just swum anyway. Go out for a pizza or something?"

Grace pulled a face. "That'd be a real waste of such fantastic weather," she said.

Jenna shrugged. "You can't have everything," she said. "'You pays your money and you takes your choice.' That's what my mum always says."

Grace gave her a playful shove. "Stop it!" she said. "You and Matt – you sound like my gran."

"Who right now is snoozing in a deckchair outside your house," said Jenna, "so I'd advise you to shut up. Look!"

"Bother," said Grace. "I can do without her right now."

"When can you do *with* her precisely?" giggled Jenna.

"When she comes bearing bodysuits," said Grace.

They strolled up the remainder of the lane as slowly as they could.

"Let's say we're off down to the village for an ice cream," said Grace.

"Fine by me," said Jenna.

But it wasn't fine by Grace's dad. When they slipped into the house to dump Grace's swimming kit, he was waiting for them.

"Grace, I want a word with you," he said. His voice was surprisingly stern. "And you, Jenna, if you don't mind."

"Can't it wait?" Grace said. Her pulse was racing but she managed to keep her voice casual. "We want to get an ice cream before the shop shuts."

"The vans will be there until dark tonight, Grace. You know that. Which makes me think there must be some truth in what your gran's just told me."

Grace gripped the back of a chair. Jenna assumed her wide-eyed innocent look.

"What's that then?" said Grace. "Not that I've been seen with a boy?"

"Don't be silly, Grace." Her father's voice was tense and his hands mimicked hers, locked around the back of the other chair. "You know that she knows you're going out with Nik."

"What then?"

"She's friendly with Mrs. Potts, your old schoolteacher. Well, not friendly exactly, but they meet at the over-sixties club. Mrs. Potts was enquiring after your health. She'd seen you at the doctor's apparently. So your Gran's been asking me, Grace. Why do you need to see a doctor? Why haven't I told her that you're poorly? And I didn't know what to say, Grace, because..." Here Grace's dad's eyes grew so bright she wasn't sure if she was seeing fury or tears. "Because I didn't know!"

There was a difficult silence.

"Mr. Hornby, it was me seeing the doctor," said Jenna. "I've been having a few problems...you know, like girls do."

"Nice try, Jenna," said Grace's dad, his face grim. "But Mrs. Potts heard Grace's name called out. And I rang your mum as soon as my mother told me – just to check Mrs. Potts hadn't made a mistake. And your mum didn't know anything about any trip to the doctor's either."

"It was still me!" protested Jenna. "I just didn't want to bother her. She fusses too much anyway."

"No, it wasn't, Jenna," said Grace, wearily, "but thank you for trying. It was me, Dad. I needed to see a doctor and I'm really sorry because you're not going to like this but I'm not going to tell you why I went and you can't make me!"

The last words came out in a rush. There was a brief, stunned silence in which it was hard to tell who was more shocked, Grace or her dad. Then Grace snatched up her towel and swimsuit and fled from the house, narrowly avoiding crashing into her gran's deckchair.

"Just where d'you think you're going to in such a tearing hurry?" demanded Gran.

"Anywhere to get away from you!" Grace hurled at her and went skittering off down the road.

"Grace!" her father roared after her, running out onto the grass in front of the cottage. "Grace! Come back! I'm sorry!"

"Robert, control yourself!" said his mother. "Sorry, indeed! What have you to be sorry for? How dare she speak to me like that? How dare she run off when you're talking to her? Sorry? Sorry? You're too soft with her, Robert, that's always been your problem. You were too soft with that wife of yours too, always letting her have her own way. And look where that got you!"

Robert Hornby turned to his mother. His face had the gritty quality that rocks had in his own paintings. He held out his hand to his mother and helped her from the chair.

"I think you've said quite enough, Mother," he said. "I'm taking you home."

She didn't argue but Jenna, caught in her ferocious glare, felt a sudden, giggly urge to hold up crossed fingers to ward off the evil eye. But really there was nothing to laugh at. Grace had always got on so well with her dad. For Jenna, there would be trouble with her mum when she got home because of the doctor's appointment but she was used to that. Grace would be devastated to have rowed with her dad and been so rude to her gran. There was only one thing to do. Jenna picked up her bag and ran down the road after Grace.

Grace went to Matt's. It was a double bluff. If her father went looking for her, he'd think she'd avoid Matt's; it was too obvious. She planned rapidly as she raced down the road. She wasn't going to return home until after she'd been out with Nik. If she did, there'd be a scene and either her dad wouldn't let her go out that evening or she'd be in too much of a state to want to. She'd meant to spend some time washing and blow-drying her hair in readiness for her date but Nik would just have to take her as he found her. If he really liked her, he shouldn't mind.

She blew her nose and rubbed at her face. If anyone commented, she'd say she'd caught the sun and her eyes were a bit sore from too much swimming. Then she pounded on Matt's back door. She knew he'd be in because there was a test match on.

"Grace!" said Matt, when he'd finally dragged himself away from the TV to answer her. "What's happened?"

The sun story evaporated. The next moment Grace was sobbing against Matt's chest and he was holding her awkwardly with one arm and stroking her hair with his free hand.

"Are your mum and dad in?" Grace gulped, suddenly panicking.

"No – they've gone off looking at garden furniture – and all the B&B-ers are out for the day, thank goodness. Come on," he said, letting go of her reluctantly. "I'll make you a cup of tea and you can tell me what's wrong."

"I can't tell you all of it," Grace sobbed. "I've had a row with my dad, that's all."

"About Nik?"

Grace shook her head. "I'm sorry, Matt, I just can't tell you."

Matt paused as he reached for the kettle. "You're not pregnant, are you?"

Grace let out a snort of laughter and had to reach quickly for a length of kitchen roll. "Oh Matt, that's exactly what Jenna said! Why does everyone immediately think that?"

"Well, I don't know about Jenna but it was just that Mrs. Potts told Mum she'd seen you at the doctor's – so Mum asked me if I knew what was wrong. I was just putting two and two together."

"Oh good grief, is Mrs. Potts going to put it on the TV news?" said Grace, wiping her eyes. "It was her that told Gran and Gran told Dad and that's why we had the row."

"So it's why you went to the doctor that you can't tell me?" said Matt.

"Got it in one."

"But you're not pregnant?"

"Matt, I'm only fourteen! What d'you think I'm like?"

Matt dumped a couple of tea bags in the pot, carefully avoiding looking at her.

"You never know," he said. "Especially with someone like Nik."

"Matt! I'm under age!" said Grace. "Nik knows that. And anyway, I wouldn't want to go that far. Honestly, we haven't got past kissing yet!"

"Right," said Matt, lifting the kettle to pour. "But if he starts giving you any hassle, just tell him he'll have me to deal with, okay?"

"Matt!" exclaimed Grace. "You can't say that!"

"I just did," said Matt.

"But you've got no right! It's up to me what I do with Nik!"

"I know...I know, don't get your knickers in a twist. I only meant if he started hassling you. You know...do this or I'll dump you. That sort of thing. Any of that and he'll wish he never set eyes on you."

Grace spluttered over the tea he'd just handed her. "Matt, stop it! You're making me choke. I always thought you were such a nice, kind, gentle person."

"Not when it comes to anyone messing you about," said Matt fiercely. "Then I make the Terminator look like a pussy cat, okay?"

For a moment, their eyes locked. Then Matt shrugged and laughed. "Oh, okay, I'm joking," he said. "Well, sort of. He's only history if he actually gets you pregnant. Anyway, what are you going to do now? Watch the cricket with me?"

"I can't wait," said Grace. "No – I don't know really. Could I make a sandwich or something? I'm starving."

"Fine. What d'you want in it?"

"I'll make it myself," said Grace. "Just tell me where everything is. You go and watch the cricket. I don't want to spoil your afternoon."

"You're not," said Matt. "Honestly. Look, it'll be much quicker if I just make it. I could do with a snack myself."

Grace decided not to argue. She didn't want him going sulky on her again.

"In that case," she said. "D'you think it'd be okay if I had a shower? I've just been in the sea and my hair's disgusting."

"Go on then," said Matt, without looking at her. "Make yourself beautiful for lover-boy. You know where the shower is. I'll find you a clean towel."

\* \* \*

Matt's family had a shower by the back door. His grown-up brothers were keen windsurfers and his dad was in the lifeboat crew. It made sense for them to peel off their wet kit and jump straight in the shower. Grace had used it herself on many an occasion. It had a good, powerful spray and as the water thundered down on her, she began to relax and to plan. She would walk along the cliff path as far as she could and then cut across to the road. There was plenty of time. Then she'd surprise Nik at his house, before he set off to meet her. She would ring her dad and tell him not to worry about her and that she'd be back later. She would apologize – she *had* been rude to her gran, after all – but she wouldn't be dragged into an argument on the phone. She didn't have to tell her dad why she had gone to the doctor's – that was her business and he shouldn't pry. If he wanted to argue with her, he could do that tomorrow; this evening was too lovely to spoil.

She stood in the shower for a long time, letting the conditioner soak into her hair. She gazed down at her body. It was, she was honest enough to admit, in fantastic shape. Wet and gleaming, in the half-light of the shower cubicle, the velvety fur was barely visible. Grace ran her hands down her torso. She could hardly feel it. Perhaps, in the sea, Nik wouldn't notice? Then she remembered that she'd be wearing her bodysuit. She wasn't sure whether she was relieved or frustrated.

Matt hammered on the cubicle door.

"Shall I just dump this towel here?" he shouted.

Grace didn't fancy stepping out into the lobby naked. Supposing his parents chose that moment to return home? "Hang on," she said. "I'm turning off the shower."

She opened the door a crack and stuck out her arm without thinking about it. She heard Matt's sharp intake of breath before the towel was in her hand. She threw it round herself and cringed. No, no, no, how could she have been so *stupid?* Grace waited till she was sure Matt had gone and then stepped out into the mess of wetsuits and sailing shoes in the lobby. She looked down at her arms. Little rivulets of water ran down them, dividing and joining before dripping off her hands. In the late-afternoon sunshine that streamed through the window, the colour difference between her furry arms and bare hands was marked. It was all too obvious that Matt had stumbled on her secret.

# 7

Grace stood at the bottom of Nik's drive. Now that the moment had come to surprise him, she was nervous. She had never been inside his house, only seen it when her father had dropped him off. She knew it was huge. Would she be welcome, just turning up like this?

She took a deep breath and pushed open one of the heavy gates. There was nothing else for it. She had phoned her dad and told him what she was doing. His inability to say anything more than a few clipped words told her how very upset he was. She had the horrible feeling that he was holding back tears. Well, he would have to get over it. She wasn't doing anything bad or wicked. If anyone was in the wrong, it was her dad, prying into her private life. She had promised she would apologize to Gran. What more could she do? Nonetheless, she wasn't happy; she had never had a serious rift with her dad before. However much she tried to take her mind off it, she felt as if she was carrying around a hard little beach pebble deep in her chest. Well, two pebbles, actually. The fur pebble and the Dad pebble. Right now, she couldn't decide which weighed the heavier.

She walked slowly up the gravel drive. It was immaculate; not even a hint of a rebellious weed struggling up for air. The house was immaculate too; a new, two-storey affair replete with sea-facing windows and balconies and a wide, imposing frontage. It had been rendered and painted and was so bright white in the evening sunshine that she had to screw up her eyes.

With great trepidation, she lifted the brass knocker and let it fall. The sound seemed to thunder in the untouched silence of the house and garden. Perhaps no one was in? Grace glanced about nervously. The house was so pristine, it was as if no one was ever in. There were no cars in the drive. Maybe they'd all gone out for the afternoon? Grace glanced at her watch. Had she time to walk back and meet Nik as arranged? She'd rather that than sit on the step and wait. How desperate would that look?

She was just about to lift the knocker again when she heard movement inside the house. She had been impatient. It was barely seconds since she'd knocked. Yes, someone was coming to the door. She knew she was being peered at through the spyhole and tried to look appealing, the sort of girl whom any mother would want for her son, then waited while the someone fiddled with the locks. The door flew open.

"Grace!" said Nik. "How fantastic! Come in, come in, I'm the only one here!"

The next moment, he had pulled her over the threshold, had his arms around her waist and was kissing her urgently.

After a few moments, she pushed him away, laughing and gasping. "Nik," she protested. "Wait – I haven't even said 'Hello'!"

"Go on, then," said Nik, stroking her hair back off her face. "Say it."

Grace smiled shyly. "Hello," she said. "Don't you want to know why I'm here?"

"I don't really care," said Nik. "I'm just glad you are. I thought you were busy till later."

"I was," said Grace. "But things changed. And I wanted to surprise you." Suddenly, she realized that she didn't want to tell him about the row. She didn't want yet another person quizzing her about her trip to the doctor's – though for all she knew, Mrs. Potts had told him too. "It was a lovely evening, so I thought I'd come over. We can walk back to Thurle Bay for a swim. D'you want to get your kit?"

"What, now?" said Nik. "Straight away? Don't you want to see my room or anything?"

"Now?" asked Grace. "But it's such a lovely evening. Don't you want to go out? I can see your room another time."

"But Grace," said Nik. "My parents aren't in at the moment. Another time, they might be."

*Okay,* thought Grace. *So that's what he's thinking. Oh Grace, you are so stupid sometimes!*

But stupid, she decided, was probably the best thing to be, right now.

"Oh, I'm sure they wouldn't want me snooping round their house while they aren't in," she said. "I know my dad wouldn't. He'd think that was really rude."

"But *I'm* here," said Nik, a flicker of impatience in his voice. "It'd hardly be snooping if I took you to my room."

"But it isn't your house, Nik," said Grace. "It's theirs.

And anyway, my dad wouldn't want me going in a boy's bedroom with no one else at home. I mean, I know you wouldn't try to do anything you shouldn't, Nik. I know you'd just be showing me, but I'd still better not. I'd feel bad about it."

Nik's face fell. "Surely your dad wouldn't mind if you just had a quick look?" he persisted.

Grace shook her head. "No, really. I'd rather not. I wouldn't feel right about it. Come on – you get your kit and I'll wait here. I'm longing to get down to the beach; it's such a gorgeous evening."

"Oh, all right then," said Nik. "Back in a minute."

Grace smiled to herself. Round one to her. Nik had nothing to fear from Terminator Matt at present. It was frustrating though. It was quite true that her father would be horrified by the thought of her alone with Nik, in his bedroom, but she was tempted nonetheless. Tonight, on the beach, in the twilight, maybe she would risk just a little more than a kiss. For now, however, they would both have to wait.


Grace enjoyed the walk back from Nik's house. They strolled along the cliff path, chatting about this and that. She was relieved that Nik seemed content with nothing more than holding her hand. Perhaps her reluctance to follow him to his bedroom had warned him off.

"Fancy a burger?" asked Nik when they reached the village. "I'm starving."

"Oh, yes please," said Grace. "So am I."

They sat close together on the wall of the beach café, eating their burgers and chips, watching the families, the surfers and sailors enjoying the last of the day's heat.

"I'm surprised you weren't out sailing today," said Grace.

Nik pulled a face. "I'm not that mad keen actually," he said. "It's all right but it's my mum and dad who are crazy about it really. That's what they were doing this afternoon. What about you? D'you like sailing?"

Grace shook her head. "Not particularly. My dad does. And he likes to row out and fish. But I just want to be *in* the water all the time. It seems crazy to be perched just above it when you could be in it. Really unnatural."

Nik leaned over and kissed her lightly on the cheek. "You're funny," he said. "It's not as if the British sea is that enticing. It's usually freezing cold for a start. I've never known anyone be as keen on it as you. I bet you still want to swim tonight, don't you?"

Grace looked startled. "Of course!" she said. "Don't you?"

"See!" he said. "How weird is that? You've already been

swimming this afternoon. Isn't that enough for one day?"

Grace shook her head fiercely. "Not for me," she said. "I'd be in there all the time, if I could!"

"Seriously? Wouldn't it get a bit boring?"

"Oh okay, then," she said. "Not all the time." She was choosing her words carefully. If she told him that she could never get bored of the sea no matter how long she stayed in and that every time she got out it was a real effort, he would think she was seriously bonkers. "I'd like to be in it more than I am though. Sometimes I worry about the future – you know, if I go to college, or something – somewhere that's a long way from the sea. I don't think I could. Once I had flu and I couldn't swim for a whole week – I thought I'd go mad!"

"Only a week?" said Nik. "If you had the flu, I'm surprised you were swimming after a fortnight!"

"Oh, the doctor said I shouldn't, of course. I felt as soggy as a jellyfish when I first went in – but Dad came with me and checked that I was all right."

"What – your dad let you, even though the doctor said you shouldn't?"

Grace nodded. "Yes, I know. Jenna's mum gave him a really hard time about it. But the thing is, Dad understands how important it is to me. He's not that keen on swimming himself so it just shows how special he is.

He knew I was going crazy, cooped up in the house. He knew it was more important for me to get in the sea than to do what the doctor said – I don't know how but he did. And he was right. I felt so much better once I was swimming again."

"But you could have got pneumonia and died!" said Nik. "It was pretty stupid, if you ask me."

Immediately, Grace bristled. "No, it wasn't! I told you – I was going mad! Dad understood that!"

"Don't be silly, Grace," said Nik. "You wouldn't have gone mad, just from not swimming! You shouldn't let it get to be an obsession – now that really would be mad!"

Grace scrunched up the paper around her burger, stood up and dropped it in the bin. Suddenly, she wasn't hungry any more.

"You don't understand," she said, coldly. "But my dad does."

Nik grabbed her arm. "Don't get cross, Grace," he said. "I'm worried about you, that's all. Your whole life seems to revolve around your next swim. Don't you ever want to go to the cinema or out for a pizza or down the bowling alley or anything?"

"Sometimes," said Grace, lying. "But while it's the summer, what's wrong with the beach and the sea?"

"Only that it can get a bit boring, that's all."

"Boring? But I'm never bored!" protested Grace. "Well, except at school, of course."

"I didn't mean just boring for you," said Nik. "I meant boring for me."

Grace's face flushed. "You don't have to go out with me," she said. "If you're bored, we can finish."

Nik's grip on her arm tightened. "Don't be like that, Grace," he said. "I'm not bored with *you* – I'm just a bit bored with swimming. With the beach. With Thurle Bay. I'd like to take you out somewhere else sometime."

Grace battled with herself. The truth was that she had barely any interest in going to any of the places he had mentioned; she knew that made her odd. Jenna and Matt told her so frequently. But they had grown up with her and took her as they found her. Sometimes she went out with them; sometimes she didn't. They didn't hold it against her. But now she stood staring down a long dark tunnel of possible boyfriends who simply couldn't understand. They would want her to compromise and she could see that was how relationships worked. She couldn't have everything her own way. The realization filled her with dread. Suddenly, there were three cold, hard pebbles in her chest.

"Okay then," she said, smiling at Nik. "Next time we'll go somewhere else. But tonight, can we still swim, please?

It's such a beautiful evening."

"Fine," said Nik. "But shouldn't we wait awhile? We've just eaten."

"We'll be okay by the time we've walked over to the bay," said Grace. "Come on. Let's go."

Even Nik had to admit it was a blissful evening to swim. Thurle Bay was almost deserted and the sun-baked water was surprisingly warm. Nik was nervous about swimming beyond the headlands into the open sea but Grace insisted that it was safe.

"If you get tired, I'll drag you back," she said. "Trust me – I can do it."

They raced against each other, somersaulted and surface dived until the sun began to go down. Then Nik swam up close to Grace and, treading water, slipped his arms around her waist. He kissed her.

"Come on," he said. "Let's go back now. I'm tired."

"Just five more minutes..." Grace began to say but a strangled yelp from Nik interrupted her.

"Grace, stay still!" he gasped. "There's a huge great seal behind you!"

Grace glanced over her shoulder. "Oh, her!" she said. "Don't worry. She won't bother us. Seals aren't dangerous anyway. Well, except the males sometimes in the mating season."

"Are you sure?" said Nik, his eyes scanning the water around them, "because we're surrounded."

Grace laughed. "Wow! They don't normally come so close. It must be because you're with me. Maybe they think you're a threat."

"Oh great!" said Nik. "What do I do? Wave a white flag?"

"Don't be silly. I mean, they think you're a threat to me. Usually, I'm here alone. They haven't seen you before."

The seals weren't coming any closer but they weren't going away either.

"Are you sure they're not dangerous?" said Nik. "How do you tell them I'm not a threat? Because could you tell them I'm not pretty quickly – I'm feeling a bit threatened myself!"

"Silly! I don't speak seal!" laughed Grace. "Come on, we'll just swim back to the beach. They'll go away soon. They live on the end of the headland. They won't come near the beach."

But Grace was wrong. As they struck out for home, the seals followed them. They didn't come any closer, the nearest ones staying a couple of metres away, but they didn't back off either.

"I thought you said they wouldn't follow us," said Nik,

his face red with the exertion of swimming hard after an hour or so in the water.

"They never have before," said Grace. "They must be curious about you, that's all. It's all right. You don't have to swim so fast. They won't hurt you, I promise."

"I'm not so sure," said Nik. "The sooner I'm back on land, the happier I'll be."

As they reached the shallower waters, the seals hung back. Whatever it was that had troubled them, they weren't going to risk landing on the beach. Grace found the gap in the rocks first and called to Nik to follow her. Once they were through, the seals turned and began to swim away.

Grace stood on the waterline watching them.

"How very odd!" she said. "Honestly, they've never done that before. It *must* have been because you were with me – I can't think of any other explanation. I'm sorry, Nik. I hope you weren't really scared."

"Well, they make quite some bodyguard," said Nik, relief making him giddy. "I certainly wouldn't risk anything with that lot around."

Grace grinned. "Oh, that's what you had in mind, was it?" she said, stretching up and kissing him lightly.

Nik made a grab for her but she slithered away and ran off up the beach.

"I'm going to get dry," she shouted over her shoulder. "Don't you dare try to watch!"

A few minutes later, Grace was dressed and ready to walk up to the cottage. She wasn't looking forward to it; however her dad reacted, it wasn't going to be easy. The evening had been lovely; maybe if she just stayed out a bit later, her dad would go to bed and she wouldn't have to face his displeasure until the morning.

Nik emerged from behind the rock where he had been changing.

"Well?" he said. "Do you have to rush back or have we got a bit longer?"

Grace smiled. "Oh, a bit longer, I think," she said. The beach was empty now. It was almost dark. She sat down on the warm sand and wasn't surprised when Nik followed suit.

"You're so beautiful," Nik murmured, putting his arm round her. "I've never met anyone with such fabulous eyes." Then he was easing her down onto her back and kissing her. Grace wrapped her arms round him, running her hands up and down his back, enjoying the taste of his salty lips and the warmth of his body against hers. His kisses became more urgent and probing and suddenly she felt as if her tongue had taken on a different life, tingling with brand new nerve endings. The excitement seemed to sizzle down into her whole body and she found that her fingers were tentatively lifting Nik's shirt, seeking the bare flesh of his back just as his, more urgent, were beginning to pull up her T-shirt.

Grace gasped, grabbed at her top with one hand and pushed Nik away with the other.

"What? *What?*" said Nik.

"Sorry...sorry, Nik," said Grace, tossing her hair out of her eyes. In that split second, she saw something, something which made her sit bolt upright with a small scream.

Nik, flung aside by the strength of her movement, rolled in the sand.

"*Grace!*"   he said. "What is it? I wasn't going to do anything! I was only..."

"It isn't that," panted Grace, her huge eyes staring. "There was someone there. Someone watching us."

"*Where?*"   said Nik. "The creep. Where is he? He can't have gone far."

"I don't think it was a man. I couldn't quite tell. And anyway, they've gone now." Grace was breathing more steadily. "Sorry – sorry – maybe I imagined it."

Nik put his arm round her. "Grace, you're shivering! What did you see? Tell me!"

Grace shook her head. "It was probably my imagination," she said. "Sometimes I have dreams like it. A tall figure, wearing some sort of loose garment – I don't know, a robe of some sort, with long hair. That's what I saw."

"A local hippy?" suggested Nik. "Is there anyone like that around here? The sort of person who might be out 'communing with nature' or whatever they do?"

Grace laughed shakily. "Only me and my dad, I think," she said. "And it certainly wasn't my dad. Don't worry, Nik. It was probably nothing. Honestly, I do have dreams like that. I probably saw some sort of shadow and my brain played a trick on me."

"Even so, I think I'd better take you home," said Nik. "You're still shaking. And don't start worrying about getting your dad to take me back. I'll ring my parents now. One of them'll be there by the time I get down to the village."

Nik phoned quickly, then picked up their bags and helped Grace up. She was glad of his warmth as he wrapped his arm round her. She had tried to make light of it but she was lying. Someone had been watching them, she was sure. As she sat up and screamed, the someone had melted away into the darkness. There were enough rocky places to hide in Thurle Bay. Whoever it was, was probably still down there. Either that, or following them. But that's how she always felt after her dreams – how she had felt that night when she thought someone had followed her up the cliff path. There was certainly no one around now – and Nik thought she was quite peculiar enough as it was. The sensible thing was to laugh it off.

Matt watched jealously as Grace and Nik, arms huddled around each other, climbed the path to the cottage. Then he stood up. He was still and cramped from sitting in his vantage point. He shook out his gangly limbs and his baggy sweatshirt billowed in the light breeze that had whipped up. He ran his fingers through his long hair and rubbed his eyes, which were tired with peering out into the darkness. He didn't think she'd seen him. No, he had been too quick for that. *So far, so good,* he thought and set off for home.

# 8

All the time Jenna was searching she suspected that Grace was at Nik's. Eventually she plucked up the courage to tell Grace's dad and returned to the cottage. Robert Hornby was pacing the kitchen, Grace's mobile in his hand.

"Why doesn't she use this wretched thing?" he demanded. "She never seems to take it with her."

"It's not much use when you're swimming," said Jenna, "but it'll have Nik's number on it and I bet anything that's where she's gone."

Right on cue the house phone rang and Robert dropped the mobile in his rush to answer it.

Jenna waited, biting her nails, trying to guess what Grace was saying.

Robert slammed the phone back into its receiver. Jenna jumped. He was such a gentle person that she was shocked by his violence.

"You were right," he said, tight-lipped. "She's gone to that boy Nik's."

Then he slumped down at the table. "I'm not used to this," he said. "Grace has never been any trouble."

"Teenagers are supposed to be difficult, Mr. Hornby," said Jenna. "It's a well-known fact. My mum says I'm a nightmare."

Robert smiled up at her wearily. "I'm sorry, Jenna," he said. "I shouldn't be burdening you with my troubles."

"Grace is my best friend, Mr. Hornby," said Jenna. "I'm worried too. Shall I make us a pot of tea?"

"That would be lovely," said Robert. "I guess I'd better think what to do when she gets back. I don't really know where to start. D'you think I should have a word with your mum?"

Jenna shook her head hard. "Don't get me wrong, Mr. Hornby," she said. "My mum's great as mums go – but she wouldn't understand about Grace. Really she wouldn't.

And I promise on my honour that Grace hasn't done anything wrong. Apart from being rude to her gran, of course."

"And lying about going to the doctor's," said Robert.

"Well...yes...that too," said Jenna. "But it is very difficult for her. Very embarrassing."

"So you know why she went?"

Jenna looked at the floor. "Well, yes, I do. Sorry."

"So she can tell you but she can't tell me?"

Jenna met his eyes unhappily. She could see how hurt he was. "Mr. Hornby, it isn't something that's easy to explain to a man. I'm sure if her mum was here, she'd tell her. It's that sort of thing. Girls' stuff."

Mr. Hornby nodded. "I guessed that. It's my own fault if I'm hurt then, isn't it? I shouldn't have driven her mother away."

Jenna felt her eyes beginning to smart. His voice was so desolate. He was such a nice man. She'd often thought how lucky Grace was to get on so well with him. Her own dad was all right, but so distant, often working away and interested in little about her beyond how well she was doing at school. It didn't seem fair for Mr. Hornby to be so upset. How could he have driven Grace's mum away? He was too kind and sensitive a man for that.

"Let's have that cup of tea," Jenna said. "I'll put the

kettle on. Then I'd better go home. My mum'll be getting worried about me."


When Jenna had gone, Robert wandered into his studio. When Grace phoned, she had apologized for her rudeness to her gran and for lying about the doctor's. She had said she never meant to upset him. She had explained that she was with Nik, that she would be back late, that it would probably do them both good to have a bit of space from each other and that he mustn't worry about her. She had behaved like the model daughter. All right, they had had an argument and she had stormed off but she had thought things through, made her apologies and built her bridges. He knew he should be proud of her. How much more mature could he expect a daughter to be? Even the trip to the doctor's could be seen as a sign of wisdom and maturity. It was just that inside, Robert felt like a little boy whose best friend has just kicked him – uncomprehending, hurt and desperately needing to cry. He wanted someone to comfort him but he had nobody. Grace was his only comforter and she was the one who had wounded him. Anyway, how pathetic was that – a grown man looking to his daughter for help? He made himself sick. He would pull himself together and work until she came home. He was an adult; he had no excuse to hang around all evening feeling sorry for himself.

Robert scanned the work he had in progress and picked up a paintbrush in readiness. Then he put it down again. On an impulse, he pulled out a large sheet of sketching paper and clipped it to an easel. He grabbed his pot of charcoal and, before he had chance to change his mind, began to draw.

When Grace let herself quietly into the cottage, she was surprised to find the kitchen in darkness. Maybe her dad had gone to bed after all. Maybe her telephoned explanation had been more soothing than she had thought. Then she noticed the strip of light gleaming under the studio door. She was tempted to tiptoe past and leave facing her father until the next day but that would be both mean and cowardly. She knew that he preferred to work in the morning. He had waited up for her and would want to know that she was home. Slowly, she pushed open the studio door and stared, open-mouthed, at the drawing on the easel.

"Dad..." was all she managed to say before her father had whisked the drawing off the board and crumpled it in his hands.

"Dad...no," she cried. "No...it was beautiful..."

Her father wouldn't meet her eyes. "It was nothing," he said. "I was just filling time – messing about. Waiting for you. Now you're home, you'd better go to bed."

His arms were folded, his shoulders hunched. He was completely closed to her. Grace wanted to cry. She would rather he shouted at her or hit her even, than this. She needed to know that he had forgiven her and that everything was all right between them – that he didn't mind that she couldn't tell him what was wrong. But everything wasn't all right and he *did* mind and nothing she could say or do was going to change that.

"Night-night then, Dad," she said, turning away. "You didn't need to wait up for me. I'm sorry."

"Night-night, Grace," said her father. "I hope you had a good evening." Then he turned back to his easel and clipped up a fresh sheet of paper.


Grace woke up screaming, hugging her sheet against her, protecting her body from the hands, Nik's hands, the watcher's hands, she didn't know whose hands, which were trying to strip off her bodysuit.

"No, no, no!" she shrieked. "Leave me alone...I don't want to...you mustn't...I..."

"Grace! Grace! Listen to me! You're dreaming! It's me – Dad!"

Grace struggled upright, the sheet still clutched around her.

"Dad?" she gasped. "Dad, is that you?"

Grace's father tried to wrap his arms around her but she still held him off.

"Yes, Gracie, it's me," he said. "You were having a terrible nightmare."

Grace took a couple of deep breaths, battling to calm herself. "Okay," she said. "Okay – I'm sorry. I'm fine now."

"No, you're not, your teeth are chattering," said her dad, unfurling the quilt from the foot of the bed where it lay folded.

Grace huddled it around herself gratefully. "It's so chilly in here," she said. "Like there's a breeze blowing in off the sea."

"You're imagining it," said her dad. "It's a really warm night. It's the shock of the nightmare that's making you shiver." He sat on the bed and looked into her eyes. "Gracie, are you all right now or d'you want me to stay with you?"

Grace snuggled down under the bedclothes. "I'm all right, Dad, honestly," she said. "Sorry – it must be because I got so worked up earlier."

Her dad nodded and tucked her in gently. "It wasn't a great day, was it? Now go to sleep, my darling. Remember that whatever happens, I'll always love you."

"Me too," Grace whispered, her voice choked.

Her dad stooped and kissed her forehead. "Sweet dreams then, Gracie," he said and crept away.

Tears ran down Grace's face and onto her pillow. She could taste them on her lips. They must account for the salty, sea scent in the room. And it was her dad who had woken her from the dream. It was her dad's hands that had felt so real. There had been no one else there. There couldn't have been.


Robert lay awake till dawn, going over what Grace had been screaming. "No, no, no!" she had shrieked. "Leave me alone...I don't want to...you mustn't." Mustn't what? It was obvious, wasn't it? She had been alone for hours with that boy Nik and had woken up screaming and clutching the bedclothes round herself. And she'd been to the doctor's and wouldn't tell him why. Surely there was only one explanation? But Grace was under age. Did doctors prescribe contraceptives to girls who were under age without telling their parents? He had a feeling that they did. He seemed to remember some controversy about it.

But what could he do? Confront Grace? Confront the boy? He blenched at the thought of doing either. What if he was wrong? All he had to go on was the visit to the doctor and a bad dream. If he was wrong, he dreaded to think what the new unpredictable Grace would do. And there was no one he could ask for advice; he was too embarrassed to ask either Jenna's or Matt's mum.

At last, worn out with worry, Robert fell into a restless sleep in which he dreamed of his long-lost wife. When he woke, he was still exhausted.

Grace thought it would be tactful to stay around the cottage the next day. Her dad, however, told her he was going to walk along the coast for an hour and do some sketching. He had a headache and hoped the fresh air would clear it. Grace immediately felt dreadful. Her father rarely suffered from headaches. She blamed herself – stress, followed by a broken night.

"Can I come with you?" she asked. "I feel pretty rotten too."

Her dad smiled. "No, love. You know you'd be better off swimming if you're feeling rough. And anyway, you don't want to be stuck with an old codger like me. Why not give Jenna or Matt a ring?"

*Not Nik, of course,* thought Grace. *He still doesn't like Nik.*

When he'd gone, Grace cut bread for toast and put the kettle on. She felt worn out but was sure she'd perk up after some breakfast and a swim. Then maybe she *would* phone Jenna or Matt. She didn't think she'd call Nik. Her feelings last night as she'd lain in the sand with him had scared her. She was almost glad of the fright from whoever or whatever had been watching them. It had cut short a difficult moment. Suddenly, she hadn't been sure how intimate she wanted to be with Nik – she still wasn't sure how much she liked him as a person. They got on well enough, of course, but she couldn't imagine sharing anything important with him – not like she could with Matt or even Jenna. For a moment, she wondered how it would have been if she had run to Nik immediately after the row with her dad. It wasn't easy. It had felt fine to cry onto Matt's shoulder, to ask him for food and to use his shower. It wouldn't have been like that with Nik. She'd have been embarrassed. And he would have just wanted to kiss her. For a split second, she imagined Matt kissing her, Matt reaching down to pull up her T-shirt. Her cheeks flamed scarlet and her hands flew up to her face. What was she *thinking* of? Matt was her *friend*; she'd known him since she was a baby. And she was going out with *Nik!*

Just then, the phone rang. Grace leaped to answer it.

"Grace? It's Matt. I was just ringing to ask if you're okay now. Did you sort things out with your dad?"

Grace felt as if her whole body was blushing. What would Matt think of her if he knew what had just been running through her mind?

"Oh...err...well, everything's sort of okay," she stammered. "Dad's got a headache and has gone off for a walk but apart from that..." She staggered to a halt. What was she saying? Everything wasn't all right at all.

"Grace? Grace? Are you still there?"

"Err...yes."

"Grace, you don't sound too good. Shall I come round?"

Grace leaned against the wall, cradling the receiver. A treacherous tear trickled down her cheek. Right then, of all the people in the world, apart from her dad, Matt was the one whom she wanted. He was the nearest thing she had to a brother or sister, after all.

"Would you?" she said, wiping her face on the back of her hand. She battled to keep her voice steady. "It'd be great if you could."

"No problem. Be there in a few minutes."

Grace put the phone down and made a pot of tea. She considered rushing upstairs to get dressed but she didn't feel like it. All the energy she had summoned seemed to have evaporated. Matt wouldn't care if she was in her dressing gown anyway. He'd seen her look far worse than this.

She was munching toast and already beginning to feel a bit better when he arrived. He let himself in, sat down, tossed back his mane of red hair and settled with his elbows on the table, chin in his hands.

"Go on, then," he said. "Reveal all."

Grace giggled. "Certainly not," she said.

"Well, reveal what's rattled your cage, then," he said. "If it's that scumbag, Nik, then just point me in the right direction."

"Well, it's not. It's dad. And, Matt, it's another dream." Grace put down her toast. The memory of the salt taste was back in her mouth, back in her nose.

"Uh-oh," said Matt. "Another dream, eh? What about this time?"

"Hands," said Grace. "Not frightening hands. Gentle hands. But Matt – they were so real! They were stroking me and I was so happy. I was lying on the beach on someone's lap and the hands were stroking me...but then...well, then they turned into Nik's hands and..."

"Stop right there. Too much information," said Matt.

Grace pulled a face at him. "Silly! That's when I woke up. I was shouting at him to stop..."

117

"Shouting at him to stop? Why?" demanded Matt. "What was he doing?"

Grace realized her mistake. She had been shouting at Nik to stop because of her fur – but she couldn't tell Matt that. Or could she? He knew, didn't he? Since yesterday, he knew. Or did he? How could she be sure that he'd seen?

"Matt, I..." Grace hesitated. "Matt," she said. "There's something very strange about me. I don't know if you know or not. That's what the dream was about."

Matt stopped lounging on the table and sat up. "I know, Grace," he said. "I know there's something strange about you. It's all right. I'll always be your friend. You can trust me."

Grace breathed a huge sigh of relief. So he *had* seen. She gave a little shudder of laughter. She hadn't realized how much it had been worrying her. She felt so much better knowing that she didn't have to hide the problem from either of her best friends. If only she could pluck up the courage to tell her dad.

"The dream though, Grace," said Matt, interrupting her thoughts. "Was it like the others? Did it have the smell and everything like the birthday dreams?"

"Yes," said Grace. "Yes, I'd forgotten for a minute. Yes, I could smell the sea and there was this strange chill in the air – *just* like the birthday dreams. Why? You look worried. It is odd, I know, but I guess it's just because the dreams are so vivid."

"I don't know," said Matt, shaking his head. "But I guess it would figure, given the way you are."

Grace stood up. "Would you like some tea?" she said. "I forgot to ask."

Matt shook his head. "How about a swim?" he said. "While it's quiet. You always feel better after a swim. And if there's only me with you, you won't have to wear that stupid bodysuit, will you?"

Grace smiled straight into his eyes. Her spirit felt lighter at the very thought. "No, Matt," she said. "I won't, will I?"


Grace couldn't believe how free she felt being back in the water in just her swimsuit. She surged way out beyond the bay, leaving Matt trailing in her wake. Then, giddy with the joyous feel of the water on her skin, she swam to the end of the headland where the seals were basking in the morning sunlight, wriggled out of her costume and draped it on a rock. She dived deep, deep down into the water, her skin tingling with the chill of the depths where the sun hadn't reached. She burst to the surface, flinging her hair back with a great yell of exhilaration and then glanced round for Matt.

He was waving his arm and shouting at her.

"Come back, Grace! Come back!" he was calling. Grace couldn't understand why. He knew she wasn't in any danger from either the sea or the seals. Then she noticed a lone figure on the beach. Maybe that was what he was worried about. Quickly, she swam back to the headland to retrieve her swimsuit, wriggled into it and swam towards the shore. By the time she reached Matt, he was almost purple in the face with anxiety.

"*Grace!*" he said. "I've been yelling and yelling!"

"I know," said Grace, perplexed. "But I had to go back and get my swimsuit. What's the matter? That person on the beach?"

"It's not just that..." Matt started and then stopped.

Grace rested her hand on his shoulder, treading water to keep afloat. "Matt...what is it?" she said.

"It's just...I think that person on the beach might be Nik."

Grace's jaw dropped in horror. "It can't be," she said. "How can you tell at this distance?"

"Better eyesight than yours?" suggested Matt. "Look closely. What do you think?"

They were drifting closer to the beach all the time. "Oh no, I think you're right," said Grace. "What am I going to do?"

"Swim round the headland into the village bay?" suggested Matt. "I could ring Jenna to take some clothes down for you."

"But Nik must have seen me by now," said Grace. "He'd think it was really odd if I suddenly began swimming away."

"I'll think of something to tell him," said Matt. "You're on a training swim for a gala or something. What's he want to come here for anyway, snooping around?"

"Matt, that's not fair," said Grace. "He's probably just checking I'm all right. We had a bit of a fright on the beach last night. I thought someone was watching us."

"Oh Grace," said Matt. "Not again!"

"I know, I know," said Grace. "I forgot to tell you – what with the dream and everything. Anyway, it was probably just a shadow; I'm getting really paranoid. But anyway, I screamed – it put a bit of a damper on the evening."

"I can imagine," said Matt. "Anyway, if you don't swim away now, you're never going to. Want me to ring Jenna then?"

Grace hesitated, treading water while she thought.

"No," she said, after a moment or two. "No. I can't carry on like this. If he's going to be my boyfriend, he's going to have to know what I'm like. There may be nothing anyone can do; he's just going to have to like it or lump it."

Matt didn't say anything and Grace didn't wait to change her mind. She waved to Nik and swam quickly towards the gap in the rocks. Matt hung back, watching, hawk-eyed.

"I came over to check if you were okay," said Nik, "but I can see that you are."

There was an edge to his voice which instantly irritated Grace, tired and unsettled as she was. She snatched up the towel she had left at the water's edge and wrapped it round her shoulders quickly. Suddenly, standing in front of him in nothing but her swimsuit, letting him see her fur didn't seem quite such a good idea.

"Well, I'm not okay actually," she said. "I feel pretty awful. I had a terrible dream last night so I didn't get much sleep."

"So how come you're down here with *him* so bright and early?"

"I've told you before. I love the sea. It makes me feel better."

"With him?"

"I was coming down here anyway. Matt dropped by so we came together. He's allowed to go swimming too, you know."

Grace was beginning to get chilly. Absent-mindedly, she began to rub herself down. Nik's attention was caught by the movement.

"My God, Grace!" he said. "Don't you think you should wax or something?"

Grace had a moment of complete, blind rage. "How dare you?" she spat. "Why on earth should a girl have to wax? *Boys* don't! And how dare you make personal remarks?"

She advanced a couple of furious steps towards him and he backed away, obviously thinking she was going to slap him.

"Calm down, Grace," he said. "I'm sorry – I only thought..."

"I don't care what you thought," she said. "You don't understand a thing about me. You don't understand about my swimming, my friends or my skin and I don't think you ever will – because you don't want to!"

It was Nik's turn to lose his temper. "All right, then, I don't! And I *don't* want to. You're weird, Grace – seriously weird. And if that ape in the water likes his girls hairy, then good luck to him – I don't! God – going out with you is like going out with a sodding seal! But it doesn't really matter anyway because I certainly don't want a girlfriend who two-times me!"

"I've already told you – I'm not two-timing you!" said Grace, trying to keep her voice calm.

"Well, I call it two-timing, even if you don't," retorted Nik. "We're finished."

"Good," announced Grace. "If I can't have friends and go out with you, then we certainly are finished." With that, she threw down her towel and stalked back into the water.

Nervously, Matt swam closer. For a moment, he thought Grace would swim straight past him she was going so fast, but at the last minute she brought herself to a stop, a spray of water arcing out and splattering him.

"Well?" he said.

Grace's huge eyes were luminous with fury.

"Well?" Matt said again. "What happened?"

Grace could barely bring herself to speak. "He was angry," she spat, "because I was out swimming with you! After giving me a hard time yesterday because I swim too much and he finds it boring! What does he expect? That I only swim on my own or on the rare occasions when he wants to?"

"But what about...well, you know..." Matt stammered.

"Oh *that*! He looked me up and down and said, 'My God! Don't you think you should wax, or something?' I couldn't believe it! Tactless or what? I can't believe I was lying on the beach with him last night! Urgh!" Grace shuddered. "What a creep! Has he gone? I don't want to look."

"Yeah, he's gone. Couldn't get away fast enough, I think. It's safe to get out now if you want to."

Grace said nothing. She was treading water hard but Matt saw that her shoulders were trembling.

"Grace?" he said. "Grace, are you all right?"

Tears spilled from her lashes and plopped into the sea. "No," she spat. "Of course I'm not! I thought...I thought maybe I was falling in love with him! Last night...on the beach when he..." She caught Matt's eye and smiled shakily. "Oh, I know...too much information!"

Matt patted her shoulder. "Come on," he said. "He's not worth it. Lucky or he'd be in serious danger. I'll race you back to the beach."

She nodded and immediately set off, leaving Matt trailing behind. He didn't care; he knew he would lose.

He watched Grace, metres ahead of him, step out of the water and onto the beach. Even at that distance, he could see where her velvety fur finished and her bare skin began. It didn't bother him but he knew how most boys would react – just like Nik.

Matt's heart clenched up with pity for her – pity and a

desperate, jealous need to protect her. Because she still didn't know everything, he felt sure. Only he, Matt, suspected exactly what was going on.

# 9

At school, on Monday, Grace could hardly concentrate. Her dad had been trying to behave normally at breakfast but had been cool and edgy and Jenna had been appalled to hear at the bus stop that she had split with Nik. Then there had been everyone else's whisperings and stares when Grace sat with Jenna and Matt on the journey to school. And there had been Nik to face too. She had managed a polite "Hello". He had said nothing. Consequently, despite the chlorinated water, it was a relief for Grace to don her bodysuit and go to swimming training in the lunch hour. Mr. Thomson seemed to be the only person in her life who was able to treat her normally just now. He made her work hard to compensate for the sessions she had missed and she was grateful. When she emerged from the water after a forty-minute workout, she felt relaxed and invigorated. She had a special drama workshop next, something she had been looking forward to before the events of the weekend. They had a theatre-in-education company running a workshop for them, which promised to be a bit different; whatever else, it would certainly take her mind off her troubles more than ordinary lessons.

Grace gobbled her lunch and hurried down to the drama studio where she was surprised to find a small theatre rig set up and the chairs arranged in rows in front of it. Jenna had saved her a seat and waved to her.

"Hurry up, Grace," said the teacher. "They're about to start."

"Sorry, Miss – late out of swimming training," Grace mumbled and squeezed along the row just as the lights went down. She settled into her chair and heaved a deep sigh. She hoped the show would be exciting or she had a horrible feeling that she might fall asleep.

She didn't. She found it fascinating. The show was less

than an hour long but she was amazed by the skill of the actors and their ability to remember what they were doing. With hardly anything in the way of props except a few pieces of cloth and a net, they told three traditional stories, in a way that mesmerized Grace. They twisted their bodies into boulders and waves and trees as the need arose, suggested different characters with nothing more than shifts in their body shapes and the tenor of their voices, and transformed the settings with varied lighting. Grace was entranced, all the more because one was an old sea story about selkies. The selkies were seal people. They could cast off their skins and take human form. The story went that, seeing a beautiful selkie woman one day, a man fell in love with her and determined to have her for himself – so he stole away her sealskin. That night she came crying around his cottage, begging him to give her skin back but he wouldn't because he wanted her so much. With no choice and no one else to turn to, she stayed with him and became his wife, raising his children and caring for him just as a good wife should. But all the time she longed to be back in the sea.

One day, the man returned to the cottage and found his children playing alone. Frantically, he ran to the place where he had hidden the sealskin – and found it gone.

His wife had left him; she had returned to her people. He never saw her again but occasionally, when he called to his children to come in from playing on the beach, he would think that he saw a seal, swimming close to the water's edge, its huge brown eyes watching them before it ducked under the waves and was gone.

"What a sad story," Grace said to Jenna, after it had finished and they were moving the chairs back. "But you can see where the idea came from. Seals look so human sometimes – it's their eyes."

"Some people think it was seals that people mistook for mermaids," said Jenna.

"It figures," said Grace. "The way they lounge around on the rocks would fit."

"They're a bit short on the long blonde hair," said Jenna. "Unlike you."

"I'm a bit short in the tail department though," said Grace.

"Well, you're *The Little Mermaid*, then," said Jenna. "You've traded with the witch and got a lovely pair of human legs."

"Right, quiet now, everyone," said the teacher. "Let me introduce you to the members of our visiting theatre company..."

Grace threw herself into the workshop. The young

actors had them working with the stories they had seen, creating alternative endings, capturing moments of great emotion in still pictures, considering the characters' motives for what they did. It was when they had been working on the selkie story for a while that she began to feel uncomfortable.

"Put yourself in the place of the selkie woman for a moment," said one of the actors. "In fact, let's have a volunteer. Yes, you..." He pointed to Jenna who had immediately put up her hand. "Come on – sit here, as if you're sitting on the beach. Now then, everyone. What do we think of her behaviour? She's abandoned her babies to go back to the sea. What do we want to say to her? Come on, let's hear you."

"How could you leave your little ones behind?" said someone.

"You're only considering yourself," said someone else.

"Isn't it more important to stay with your husband now?" a boy chimed in. "After all, you chose to marry him."

Grace felt a great choking sensation rising in her chest. How could they be saying these terrible things? Didn't they understand that the woman had to go back? That the sea was her lifeblood? That without it, eventually she would wither and die? She didn't want to go – of course, she didn't – she didn't want to leave her children, but she had no choice! Grace had to do something to stop the cruel voices or she thought she might explode.

"No," she protested, standing suddenly. "No – don't you understand? The man stole her skin! He forced her to stay. But she couldn't live like that for ever. It would have killed her. She wasn't an ordinary woman. She was a selkie!"

There was a stunned silence. Grace looked round at her startled peers and brushed her hand across her face. She felt slightly giddy. Jenna put a hand on her arm and pressed her back into her seat.

The young actor in charge quickly recovered the situation.

"Well done!" he said. "Exactly so – and that's where we're going next. What about the man? The man who so heartlessly kept her there against her will? Was he any better than a kidnapper? What do we want to say to *him*? Yes, you..." He pointed to a boy. "Come out and take the part of the man."

Again the voices started.

"You didn't love her, you just wanted her for sex!" said one girl.

"Pervert! You should be ashamed of yourself!" agreed another.

"Didn't you think that she might have a family in the sea?" a boy asked.

"I'm glad she left you. You got what you deserved," added Jenna.

Grace found her breath coming in hard, panicky gasps. There was a strange whirling sensation in her head. She clung to the base of her chair and tried to breathe steadily, just as she did when she was nervous before a race. She must have worked herself too hard in the pool; she felt as if she might be going to faint.

"Are you all right, Grace?" whispered Jenna. Her voice seemed to be coming from a very long way away.

"Just feel a bit odd," Grace mumbled. "I'll be all right in a minute."

But she wasn't.

"Now what about the children?" the actor was asking. "Half-human and half-selkie. Think that might cause any problems? Webbed feet perhaps? Or whiskers? Might they only be able to eat fish? What do you think?"

"They'd be very good swimmers," interrupted one boy, grinning round the class for approval. "Hey, Grace – maybe you're one!"

There was general laughter and the lesson moved on. Supposing other children found out about the half-selkie children? Supposing they started picking on them? What then? Grace barely heard any of it. The boy's smart remark had plunged her into a nightmare – here, in broad daylight, in the middle of a drama lesson. A nightmare far worse and more real than any of her dreams. She sat rooted to her chair, unable to move, great waves of nausea rising and falling in her chest. *No*, she kept telling herself, *no, don't be ridiculous. It can't be true, it's simply impossible. You're going mad, girl, get a grip on yourself.* But the truth was, the facts fitted too well. She loved the sea too much for normality; Nik had been right – it was an obsession. Her mother had disappeared long ago with no explanation and her father had never forgiven himself; the neighbours and her grandmother had thought her mother odd. Grace looked down at herself. Weren't the very clothes she was wearing proof enough? A long-sleeved shirt and trousers on a hot day because her body was covered in short, dense, velvety fur. Sealskin. That's what it was. It had to be true. Her mother was a selkie.

Grace put up her hand shakily and caught the teacher's eye.

"I'm sorry, Miss, I'm going to have to go out," she said. "I think I'm going to be sick."

*  *  *

Jenna followed her. It was the way things worked in school. Someone always went with you if you felt poorly. This time Jenna had to run to keep up with Grace who was intent on finding the nearest loo. She waited anxiously outside the cubicle as Grace retched and retched until there was nothing left.

"Grace?" she said, when Grace finally emerged. "Shall I go and ask for them to ring your dad so he can come and get you?"

Grace shook her head. "He's out somewhere working today," she lied. "I'll go home on the bus."

"Grace, you can't do that! Let me ring my mum – she'll come and get you, I'm sure. You're really ill!"

Grace shook her head. "I'll be all right now," she said. "Probably too little sleep and all that fuss with Dad. I just need to go home and get some rest. Don't worry – I'll be fine."

"But they won't let you go just like that," said Jenna. "They'll want someone to pick you up."

"Then I won't tell them," said Grace. "Really, Jenna, just let me go. You can cover for me, can't you?"

Jenna grimaced. "Have it your own way then. You'd better get going."

"Thanks, Jenna. I knew I could count on you. I'm sorry – I just need to be on my own for a while."

Jenna gave her a shrewd look. "It was that story, wasn't it?" she said. "And what that stupid git Neil said. Just ignore him – he's an idiot. Everyone knows it's just a story. No one can really be a selkie."

Grace paused and looked directly at Jenna. "Do you believe that, Jenna?" she said. "Really?"

"Of course I do, silly," said Jenna. "Honestly, Grace – you didn't for a moment think it could be true, did you?"

Grace looked at the floor.

"Oh Grace, you didn't! Honestly, I'm not surprised you were sick. Look, you can't go dashing off home because of that! Forget it – it's just coincidence. Come on – have a drink of water. It's nearly break anyway and then we've got boring old Geography. That'll calm you down."

Grace took some deep hard breaths. Slowly, the floor stopped looking as if it was coming up to meet her. *Stop panicking,* she told herself. *Get a grip! What are you thinking of? It's a story – just a story.*

She wrapped her arms round Jenna and gave her a quick hug. "Thanks, Jenna," she said. "I think I must be going mad. Too stressy a weekend. I'm not used to all this excitement."

"Too right," said Jenna. "You ought to come out more with me and Matt and everyone. Get you more used to it.

Come on now – a drink of water and a face wash, that's what you need."

Grace did as she was told. Jenna was funny when she slipped into mum-mode but today Grace wasn't laughing. Jenna must be right, of course. No one could be the daughter of a selkie; it was impossible. How ridiculous to believe even for a moment that she might be!

# 10

Grace felt fine until she was eating her tea. Jenna's no-nonsense dismissal of her fears held good till then. Her father was uncharacteristically quiet, still brooding she knew, over their dispute two days ago. She examined his face closely while he was busy eating and avoiding her eyes. He was a slight man, grey-haired and heavily lined. She knew he was forty-four but he looked at least fifty. She'd always assumed that it was his outdoor life that had aged him but supposing there was more to it than that?

She knew he blamed himself for her mother's leaving. That was normal enough – any man might. But supposing...just supposing...no, she couldn't imagine it. Not her gentle, sensitive, reclusive father. He would never force a woman to stay with him against her will.

Grace cleared her plate away and asked her dad if he'd like some tea, expecting him to sit and read for a while, as she settled down to her homework.

"No thanks, Grace," he said. "I need to get on with something in the studio."

"I can bring it through," said Grace, surprised.

"No, don't do that, please," he said. "I don't want to be disturbed. Don't worry about the washing up. I'll do it later. You'll be all right, won't you?"

"Of course."

Grace watched him pull himself out of his chair and walk across to the studio door. His shoulders seemed stiff and hunched and for the first time ever she found herself imagining him as an old man. A great rush of love and pity threatened to overwhelm her.

"Dad!" she gasped.

He turned. "What?"

"Nothing," she said. And then, "I do love you, you know."

Her dad smiled and for a moment the heavy, tired look

lifted from his face. "I love you too," he said and then disappeared into his studio.

Grace struggled to concentrate on her homework. She'd hardly done any at the weekend and needed to catch up. Her mind was completely unsettled. She kept finding herself sitting staring into space thinking, *What if? What if my mother really was a selkie? What would that make me?* Then she would shake herself back to reality, tell herself off for being so stupid and return to her work. When she finally finished, the sun was beginning to set and her dad hadn't emerged from his studio. No chance of any television then, and anyway, her skin still stank with the unnatural reek of chlorine; she needed a swim in the sea.

"Dad!" she called through the studio door. "I'm just going down for a swim."

Her dad muttered something which she took as permission so she grabbed a towel and headed for the beach. As she reached the top of the path, she heard the phone ringing but she couldn't be bothered to go back. It was probably only Jenna checking that she was all right after this afternoon – and the truth was, she was sure she'd feel much better after she'd been in the sea.

She hurried down the path and was delighted to find that, as she'd expected, the bay was deserted. She found a large rock as close to the water as possible and stripped off her clothes behind it. She peered out. The coast was clear. Her heart raced a little with the thrill of anticipation and then, completely naked, she ran across the short stretch of sand and shingle to the gap in the rocks and plunged into the water.

Bliss! That moment as the cool, salty water struck her bare skin! There was nothing like it and she hadn't felt it for so long! Years of experience had taught her the best times of day for skinny-dipping in Thurle Bay but ever since her fur had begun to grow, she had become self-conscious. Being seen naked was one thing; being seen furry was something else. Today, however, she felt reckless. She needed to feel the water against her; she needed that moment of naked impact. It was like fresh water after too much Coke, an ice pack for a throbbing head, lashing rain after a stifling afternoon. Pulling off her swimsuit in the water, as she had yesterday, just wasn't the same. She dived, deep under the surface of the waves, revelling in the touch of the sea over her whole body, stretching out her fingers and toes, opening her eyes wide and rotating her head gently so that her hair swirled out and the water lapped every pore.

She surfaced a good fifty metres from the shore and laughed to see the bobbing heads of the seals in the water. She was surrounded by them, their gentle, doleful eyes gleaming in the last of the sun's rays. As usual, one female swam slightly closer to her than the others. Today, she was so close that Grace could have reached out and touched her. She didn't; she was wary of startling her. She felt utterly relaxed and at ease out in the bay with the seals. What a wonderful life it would be! The sea to endlessly explore, none of the hassles of everyday life to worry about and no one to comment on the state of your skin. Grace lay back in the water and floated contentedly. She closed her eyes and let the waves rock her to sleep.

It was the chilly nose of a seal which nudged her awake. That's what she dreamed anyway. She woke to immediate terror, glancing round rapidly to see how far she had drifted. There wasn't a seal in sight and it was dark now but there was enough light from the moon to see that she was still just within the bay. Her body was chilled and she trod water for a few moments to loosen herself up. She felt sick with horror at what she had done. However strong a swimmer she was, allowing herself to fall asleep was insane. The sea was calm now; she was lucky. Supposing a wind had sprung up? Supposing she had slept until the tide turned? In fact, if she wasn't mistaken, it was on the turn now. She needed to swim hard, immediately, to make sure she got back to the beach safely.

Grace struck out powerfully for the shore. She was right; the tide was beginning to go out. She had no doubt that she would make it back but it was going to be tough and she had given herself a nasty fright. She could see the seals now, settled for the night on the headland. Had one of them woken her? Or had the chill in her body caused her to dream that cold, gentle nose? Whatever. Seals and selkies were the least of her worries right now. She simply had to concentrate on getting safely back.

When she finally heaved herself through the gap in the rocks and onto the beach, her teeth were chattering. Too cold and shocked for caution, she recklessly rubbed herself down and pulled on her clothes. She was still cold so she started to jog up the beach, worrying now that her dad might have finished his work and be wondering if she was all right. She had lost track of how long she had been away.

It was when she was almost at the cliff path that she began to feel watched. Had she heard something? She paused, looked round hurriedly and then jogged on. There was nothing there; she had imagined it. But the feeling didn't go away. At the foot of the path, she stopped and glanced round again, her heart beating faster with exertion and fear. Was she looking for a figure with long hair and a loose robe? She didn't know. She still couldn't be sure whether she had seen someone when she was with Nik or not. Suddenly, she heard the skitter of pebbles – but above her, not on the beach. Grace stood petrified, not knowing whether to run on up the path or stay still. The cottage was above her, not far away. If she carried on, at least there was more chance of her dad hearing her if she had to scream. The beach behind her was oppressively dark now, hiding she knew not what, as the moon dodged behind the clouds.

Grace began to scramble up the path, pebbles and sand slithering away beneath her frantic feet. She couldn't hear anything apart from her own rasping breath and the noise of her hasty progress but she still felt there was someone else there, whether in front or behind, she didn't know.

She careered round a bend in the path into blank darkness. Someone was blocking the path.

"Dad!" Grace screamed. "Dad! Help me!"

"Grace! It's all right! It's me – Matt!"

Grace collapsed against Matt's chest. "Oh God," she panted. "Oh God, I was so frightened! Matt, I've been so stupid."

Matt tried to hold her up by the elbows and then, sensing Grace's legs buckling, sat down with her on the path.

"Oh God, Matt – you were right – I shouldn't come down here on my own at night!" Grace gasped. "I've been so stressed – I just relaxed in the water and fell asleep! I was almost out of the bay when I woke up – and the tide was beginning to turn. And I was really cold and stiff. I didn't have my bodysuit on – well, to be honest, I had nothing on."

"Grace!" said Matt. "How stupid is that? Thank goodness you woke up. You could have died of hypothermia, never mind drowning. Grace, you've got to be more careful. You really have."

"I know, I know," said Grace. "I really scared myself. And then, coming back, I was sure there was someone there again – someone watching me. That's why I was so frightened when I bumped into you. It's horrible, Matt. Maybe they were watching me all the time – taking my clothes off and everything. That would fit with Saturday night – some pervert who's hanging around watching people for kicks."

She felt Matt go tense. "Come on, Grace. I don't like this," he said. "Let's get you home. Are you going to tell your dad?"

Grace shook her head. "I don't know. I mean, what is there to tell? I'm not telling him I fell asleep; he'd go demented and never let me out swimming alone again.

And as for the watcher – well, it felt so real – but then so do my dreams. It was terrifying – but how can I be sure I didn't imagine it? I mean, out there in the bay, I dreamed it was a seal that woke me up."

Matt stood up and pulled Grace to her feet. "Well, that would figure, wouldn't it?" he said. "Given the way you are."

Grace flushed. "That isn't funny, Matt," she said. "Don't ever say anything like that again, please."

Matt dropped the hand he'd held to drag her up as if he'd been burned. "I'm sorry, Grace," he said. "I thought..."

"No, you didn't think," Grace snapped. "The way I am is not something to make jokes about."

"It wasn't meant to be a joke..." started Matt, his voice puzzled.

"Matt, just leave it, all right?" said Grace.

They walked the rest of the way in silence.

"Well, goodnight then," said Matt, when they got to the cottage. "Take care. I'll see you tomorrow."

"Yeah, goodnight Matt," said Grace. "I'm sorry I snapped at you. Thanks for rescuing me."

"Any time," said Matt and walked off down the hill, whistling quietly, his long hair catching the night breeze.

Grace stood watching him for a moment. The outside light on the cottage threw his shadow up against the wall of the lane. Long hair, loose billowing hoodie. Grace caught her breath. No, no...she pushed the thought away from her. Not Matt. Matt couldn't be the creep who was watching her. But with a horrid, hard sinking feeling she realized he had offered no explanation for his sudden appearance on the path. She was beginning to lose count of the cold little pebbles she was carrying around in her heart.

# 11

When Grace entered the cottage, her dad was on the phone.

"Oh, thank goodness, she's just walked in," she heard him say. "I'm so sorry to have bothered you. Yes, I know — yes, I'll do that. Thanks. Yes. Goodbye then."

He put the phone down with such careful control that she knew that he was furious.

"Well?" he said, his voice icy-calm. "It's after eleven o'clock."

"I did tell you I was going swimming," said Grace in a small voice.

"That was nearly two hours back. I stopped working a little while ago and assumed you'd gone to bed. I went up to check and found you weren't there. Then I found that all your swimsuits were here. I didn't know what to do – ring the coastguard or check with your friends. I tried Matt and he wasn't in either – his mum said he went out to see you a couple of hours ago and she was just about to ring to tell him he should be home. Then I tried Jenna but she was in bed and her mum had no idea where you might be. Thank goodness I hadn't got as far as calling the coastguard out. What a waste of money that would have been! What's happening to you, Grace? Have you no sense of responsibility? Surely you haven't been swimming with Matt for two hours? I presume you *were* with him?"

"Yes," said Grace, blurting out the first answer that came into her head. Her brain was reeling. Matt had been out for *two hours*? It confirmed her worst suspicions. But that wasn't the point right now. She needed to cover her tracks and if Matt was claiming to have been with her, then their stories had better match, whatever he'd really been doing. "I'm sorry, Dad. We just lost track of the time." She knew it sounded lame but she couldn't think what else to say. Her brain felt too overloaded to think up something convincing. Matt – Matt, of all people, whom she had trusted with her most intimate secrets – could possibly be sneaking around after her like some kind of stalker? Surely not – not Matt? Had he got so suspicious of Nik? She was aware of her dad's eyes boring into her. He expected something more.

What should she say? What would Matt tell his mum? However big a creep he was turning out to be, it would help her if their stories tallied. "Dad, I've finished with Nik," she started, "and—"

"Now you're with Matt?" her father interrupted. "Grace, you astonish me! You've hardly finished with one boy and you've started with another? What's happened to my little girl?"

Grace's jaw dropped open. "What?" she said. "What are you talking about? I never said I was going out with Matt! Wait, Dad! Listen to me!" But her dad was in full-flow.

"What about that trip to the doctor's that you won't tell me about?" he demanded. "What am I supposed to make of that? You can tell Jenna all about it but you can't tell me – and suddenly you're going out with boys. I'm sure you know why teenage girls often make secret visits to the doctor! What am I supposed to think, Grace? Well? What?"

Grace stared at him in disbelief. "Dad, you've got it all wrong!" she cried. "Going to the doctor's got nothing to do with boys! I'm not on the pill or anything! I'm not like that. Honestly, Dad – I've done nothing more than kiss Nik – I promise! I couldn't do anything more, even if I wanted to because…" Grace stopped, tears suddenly choking her voice. She had to tell him. There was simply no other way of explaining. However horrified he was, he simply had to know. "Dad, I went to the doctor and Nik has finished with me because…because of this!"

With that, she shoved up her sweatshirt sleeves and yanked it up at the waist. "Look, Dad! Look! Wouldn't you go to the doctor if you were covered in *fur*?"

Slowly, as if he was walking on the moon, Grace's dad crossed the room. He stretched out a trembling hand and, as gently as if he were touching a newborn baby, he stroked her arm. Then, his whole arm shaking now, he brushed his fingertips across her bare midriff.

"It's all over me, Dad," said Grace, snorting back her tears. "Literally. All over. Except my face and neck, hands and feet."

Grace's father crumpled. He slumped down in a chair and buried his face in his hands.

"Oh Gracie," he sobbed. "Gracie, Gracie, my darling. What have I done?"

And then Grace knew. She knew exactly what he had done. She had heard his story only that afternoon. She knew why her mother had left, where her mother was now, why the sea felt as much her home as the land ever did and why her skin was covered in fur. Her father, whom she loved so dearly, was a bigger creep than Nik, a bigger creep than Matt was turning out to be – he was the biggest creep she had ever met in her entire life.

"How *could* you?" she shouted at him. "How could you do that to anyone? You *scum*! I hate you, I *hate* you. You ruined her life and you've ruined mine. I'm glad she left! Glad, do you hear me? You got what you deserved!"

There was nowhere to go except outside and that was where Grace went, flinging herself down the path that only a short time ago she had struggled up in such terror. Harsh sobs burst from her throat as she ran, slithering and sliding and losing her footing all the way down to the beach. She wasn't frightened. The watcher was only Matt. And her dad wouldn't follow her – how could he? He wouldn't dare!

Grace's burst of furious energy took her as far as the beach. Then she collapsed, sobbing, full-length on the sand, crying so hard that her whole body ached. Her calm, ordered, peaceful world had shattered in the space of a few weeks. She didn't know where to go or what to do. How could she live with her father, after what he had done? What had they said in the drama workshop? No better than a kidnapper. What should she do? Go to the social services? Ring ChildLine? What could she say? "I don't want to live with my dad any more because my mother is a Selkie and he forced her to marry him?" They'd think she was barking! This was just the sort of time when she needed Matt – kind, unshockable, understanding Matt – but he and her dad were a pair. They had both let her down.

So that left Jenna. Could she go to Jenna's mum and explain? Of course she couldn't. And Jenna herself? Could she help? Not judging by what she'd said that afternoon – she'd think Grace had flipped her lid. No, Matt was the only person who would believe her – and she couldn't trust him any more. She burst into a fresh storm of sobs.

Painfully, she sat up. She was cold, exhausted and gritty with sand. She wiped her face with her sleeve and stared out into the bay. How lovely it would be just to swim away from all this! Her mother had been able to change from seal to human form – maybe she could do it the other way round?

*Get a grip, Grace,* she told herself, scrambling to her feet. *If all this is true, you're only half-selkie. You can't become a seal – you're just stuck with the fur. And the crappy dad. And the creepy friend.*

She stood, shoulders slumped, gazing out to sea. Would a swim help? No – for once even that wouldn't solve anything. In any case, for the first time in her life, she knew that she was too exhausted to risk the sea.

It was then that she detected a slight movement in the darkness. She peered closely. Yes, the darkness was deeper there, just twenty or so metres away. Was it a rock? No, she knew the sand ran smoothly down to the shoreline just there. And anyway, the shape was moving, coming closer. Definitely.

"Matt?" she said, a catch in her voice. She couldn't work out why or how he came to be there but it must be him. "Matt?" she said again. "Cut this out, please. I know you're there."

The shape was coming closer. Grace's throat was dry; she couldn't speak any more. She didn't know what to do – run, hide, scream. It all seemed equally useless. Anyway, surely, surely Matt wouldn't want to hurt her? Really there was nothing to be scared of; she must just stay very calm.

"Grace," said a sad, husky, female voice in the darkness. "Grace, my darling."

Grace's fur stood on end. "Who's there?" she whispered. "Who are you?"

Standing still now, just a few steps away from her, Grace could see a slender woman with long hair, wrapped in some sort of cloak. She was reaching out towards Grace.

Grace stumbled forward. This must be a dream; it

couldn't be real. There was nothing to be frightened of. "Mother," she whispered, grasping the cold, smooth hands. "You are my mother, aren't you? You're not a ghost or anything, are you? You're a selkie."

The woman said nothing, but simply pulled Grace towards her wrapping her in the folds of her cloak, kissing and kissing her again, while tears, saltier than brine, streamed down her face.

"My darling," she said, at last. "My darling baby girl! I left you but I always swore I would come back if you needed me!"

Grace drew back. "How did you know?" she asked. "How *could* you know?" And then she remembered the seal, the one that always came closest. "Are you? Are you...?"

"Yes, my love, I'm always close at hand. I was the one who woke you this evening when you fell asleep. Your father doesn't know it but I never go far from the bay. I watch for him too, but I keep my distance; he is nervous of seals now. They don't like him. Poor Robert!"

Grace pulled away. "Poor Robert!" she said. "He deserves to be nervous! After what he did to you! I don't know what I'm going to do but I'm never going back to him! He stole your skin and forced you to marry him! He's evil!"

The selkie looked startled. "Who told you that?" she said. "Did Robert?"

It was Grace's turn to look surprised. "No..." she stammered. "No...I just assumed...something I heard... and, I mean, he always blames himself that you left...anyway, why else would you stay?"

"Because I loved him." said Grace's mother.

Grace couldn't think what to say. Why hadn't she thought of that? She had jumped to a terrible conclusion. It was the drama workshop that had done it. She had believed it, word for word. How could she have been so stupid?

Her mother was watching her carefully. "I'm only guessing," she said in her deep, husky voice, "but I'm wondering if you've been listening to any old stories?"

Grace nodded. "Yes," she said. "Yes. I heard one today. It all seemed to just click into place."

"I can see why," said her mother. "We tell the old stories too. Of course we do. They happened – many times over – until we got wise and stayed out of men's way. But that wasn't how it was with Robert. How could you think so?"

"I don't know," whimpered Grace, tears rising again in her eyes. "I've been so confused lately. Everything's been falling apart."

Her mother took her in her arms again. "Not Robert," she said. "He won't fall apart. You can trust him. I am the untrustworthy one. Come here. Let's sit down and I'll tell you our story – your story, of course. Though we should be quick. Poor Robert will be half-crazed with worry for you by now."

Tentatively, aching in every bone, Grace sat down in the sand, allowing her mother to wrap her in her cloak, intrigued to feel her skin which, unlike her own, was smooth and bare.

"It was like this," the selkie started. "I was an adventurous youngster, always pushing the boundaries. I knew the old stories and I wanted to see what men were like, even though I knew the risks. I used to swim close to yachts and surfers, eyeing up the boys. Generally, I didn't much like what I saw. They were too active, too aggressive, never taking time out to be still, always noisy and cursing. And then, one day, at the very end of the headland, I saw your father. I hadn't gone out looking. We were all simply basking on the rocks. He was painting, of course. I loved him at once. There was something about him – so peaceful, so tranquil. And his face was so sensitive. He seemed a different sort of creature entirely from the other men I had seen. From that day on, I watched for an opportunity – a chance to slip out of my skin and for him to see me as a woman. The day came, of course. He was always about, somewhere along the coastline, and it was an easy matter for me to nip away from the others and to find him alone. I was crafty. I waited till he was crossing a tiny bay and then I slipped out of my skin behind a rock and lay in his path as if I was sunbathing – naked, of course."

"Good grief," said Grace. "It must have been a bit of a shock for him."

Grace's mother laughed. "Yes, I believe he was a little surprised – and very, very apologetic. But, he is, after all, a man. He quickly got over it, especially when I suggested that he joined me for a dip in the sea."

Grace let out a low whistle. "Phew! Are you sure this is my dad you're talking about?"

Grace's mother gave a short laugh but it was tinged with sadness. "Oh yes – I'm sure it was your dad. I've never forgotten that first time with him."

Grace waited, impatient to hear what happened next. "Go on then," she urged. "How did you come to get married?"

Grace's mother sighed. "I seduced him," she said. "I'm sorry if that shocks you. I didn't feel badly about it at the time. After all, what did I know about the way humans go about their relationships? And he was a grown man –

nearly thirty years old. He could have stopped me at any time he wanted to."

"But he didn't," said Grace.

"No, he didn't. Not then, nor all the days afterwards when we met. Not even when I told him the truth about what I was. He just said, 'I guessed, my love. I guessed as soon as I met you. I've known the old stories since I was a boy.' So you see, I wasn't entirely to blame."

"Of course not," said Grace, squeezing her hand. "Go on."

"Well, the trouble started when he wanted me to marry him, to live in a house and to be a proper wife for him. He wanted to commit his life to me – to be with me, day after day. He said we were soulmates. At first I refused. How could I live in a house all the time without my skin? But he said he couldn't live without me – that if I returned to the sea, he would follow me. He promised we would live as close to the sea as possible and that I could have my skin whenever I wanted so that I might swim with my family. But I was to live with him, not with them. He was so insistent, so desperate for me to stay. And by then, Grace, I knew that I was carrying a child. Not a seal child, a human child. I needed his help – and I wanted my child to have a father. So I married him. Maybe even then I sensed how it must end. Robert's mother was horrified, especially when you arrived far too early to have been conceived after we were married. Nor did she like our choice of home, the little cottage you still live in, so out of the way and so close to the sea. She always suspected there was something odd about me and sometimes I wondered if she knew the truth. She wasn't unkind but there was never any warmth there. And I couldn't relate to the other women in the village – their ways were so different – so hurried and unnatural. I was only ever truly happy when Robert was with me. And, of course, as time went by, he wasn't with me so much. At first I went with him on his painting trips, swaddling you up and taking you too. But as you got bigger and began to crawl, it became more and more difficult. And your grandmother was always criticizing me for following Robert around and taking so little care of the house. Gradually, I stayed at home more and then my only solace was the sea. I had taken you bathing from the moment you were born. It was the natural thing to do and you loved it. If ever you were fractious and miserable, I took you into the sea and you settled. And so you were the sweetest, calmest, happiest baby ever – but in the end, even you weren't enough for me."

A great lump had risen in Grace's throat, almost too painful to bear. "What happened?" she croaked.

"Nothing dramatic," said the selkie. "Slowly, it just got

too difficult. I was desperately lonely, desperately homesick. The love of a man and a child weren't enough for me. I was shrivelling away. I felt so tied down – as if I'd completely lost my freedom. There was never any time just to be. More and more, I found myself longing for my old life back. Robert guessed there was something wrong but I couldn't bring myself to tell him. I couldn't break his heart – I wasn't brave enough. So one day, while he was out painting, I simply asked Matt's mother if she could mind you for a couple of hours and then I returned to the sea. I knew Robert would know where I had gone. I knew he wouldn't contact the police or worry for my safety. I left him a short note – he had taught me to write, after a fashion. But he would have known, anyway. I had taken my skin."

Grace couldn't bear to listen to another word. She stood up, pulling herself away roughly from her mother.

"You broke his heart!" she burst out. "You broke his heart – and you abandoned me! How could you do that? How could you leave us behind? I don't need you messing up my life now. I never want to see you again! I wish you'd never come back."

Then she turned and ran, stumbling and tripping, back yet again, to the cottage.

# 12

Grace didn't see the dark shape blocking the path this time; she simply ran straight into it.

"No, no, no – leave me alone, Matt!" she screamed, fighting off the arms that were trying to hold her. "Dad! Dad! Help me!"

She kicked out at the shins as her father had told her to and then raised her knee, desperately trying to wound where it would hurt most.

"Grace! Grace! Stop it! It *is* me – Dad! I'm not going to hurt you. Stop fighting me!"

Grace went limp, poleaxed by the unexpected voice.

"Dad?" she quavered. "Dad? Is that...?" Of course it was. How could she have mistaken her slight, gentle father for Matt with his big bones and angular shoulders?

"Oh Dad," she whispered. She wanted to cry but she hadn't the energy. "Please take me home."

Her dad wrapped his arm around her and half carried, half dragged her back to the cottage and up to her bedroom.

When she was in bed, he drew the covers up around her and kneeled down beside her, stroking back her hair.

Grace reached up a tired hand to hold his. "Dad, I'm so sorry," she mumbled.

"You've nothing to be sorry for," he said in a choked voice. "I was the one who did everything wrong."

"Not everything," Grace whispered. "It wasn't your fault."

"Go to sleep now, my darling," said her father. "We'll talk in the morning."


Robert kneeled by Grace's bed, long after she had fallen asleep, counting her breaths, thanking God that she had returned to him. If she too had run away from him, he didn't think he could have carried on. He would have done what he had threatened all those years ago when Marina had been unsure about marrying him; he would have followed her into the sea. Marina! What a silly name he had given her! But it had seemed obvious and she hadn't cared. He should have realized then the trouble he was creating. She hadn't cared about any of the things human women seemed to care about – except for him and their baby. And in the end, even they weren't enough.

Grace shifted in her sleep, flinging an arm out across the covers. He could see the short, dense, velvety fur glimmering in the moonlight. Very delicately, he reached out and stroked it. It was so fine, so blonde. How could she think it wasn't beautiful? How could she have been so ashamed to tell him? But he knew really. It wasn't normal. Normal was what counted these days. Well, it always had. That was why he had always been a loner, picked on at school because he hated football and rugby, scorned by most girls who took him for a wimp. He had known he wasn't. He was tough and wiry, an excellent rower and strong swimmer but these things he did alone; they weren't noticed. Only his painting was noticed and even that was scorned for a long time. His parents made no secret of their concern that he would never make anything of himself. It was years before his talent was recognized and then respect for him grew. Suddenly, women found him interesting, smarming around him at launch nights for his exhibitions. But he didn't trust them. They were attracted to his successful image, not his secret soul. Not until he met Marina had he felt able to trust his inner self to anyone. He knew – he knew almost at once – what she was. His belief in the old stories was one of the things that marked him out; one of the things he knew he couldn't share with anyone else if he didn't want to end up in an asylum. To him, stumbling upon Marina, it had quickly been obvious what she was. Beautiful naked girls simply didn't lie around on deserted beaches, miles from anywhere. In any case, there was something about her eyes, something about the chill of her skin and her strong scent of the sea that gave her away and stole his heart. An ordinary woman would never understand him – but a selkie might.

And so he had let himself be carried away with the dream. The dream that here was his soulmate, the one being in the world who could make him happy. That was why he had been so desperate for her to stay and had made that terrible, unforgivable, despicable threat, that if Marina left him, he would have to follow her – to his death. How wrong he had been. How selfish. How cruel. He had almost broken her spirit but she had had the sense to run away before it was too late. Perhaps he had broken her heart instead; he had certainly broken his. And here, now, lying in the bed in front of him, was the other victim of his selfishness – Grace. Exhausted, confused, shocked, hurting – and covered in fur.

Grace finally woke the next morning because she was ravenously hungry. It was past eleven o'clock. The moment he heard her on the stairs, her father burst from his studio.

"I'll make you some tea. Sit down," he said. "I've rung the school to say you won't be in, so don't worry about that."

"I'm not," said Grace with a weak smile. "I think I've got enough to worry about."

She let her father fuss round her, burning the toast and plying her with tea, without saying anything. She felt as if she'd weathered a hurricane and been tossed up on the beach. It was another warm day but she felt chilly and pulled on one of her dad's sweaters which was lying on his chair.

Her dad watched her anxiously. "You're cold?" he said. "D'you think you caught a chill last night? Had you better go back to bed?"

"No, I'm just so tired," Grace replied. "I don't think I've

got enough energy left to bother with keeping warm. But I don't want to go back to bed. I want to be with you."

"We'll go into the studio," her father said. "It catches the morning sun." He smiled at her, the ghost of a mischievous smile. "And we'll stuff ourselves with chocolate. That should boost your energy levels."

"Sounds good," said Grace and, picking up her mug of tea, followed him across the kitchen.

At the door of the studio, her dad hesitated. Then, muttering something which sounded like, "Well, why not?" he pushed it open and let her in.

Grace gasped. Fastened up on an easel, in the middle of the room, was a picture such as she had never seen her father paint before. He rarely painted figures – only landscapes and the sea and even then his style had a bold, abstract quality which some people disliked.

The picture in front of Grace was certainly bold but there all similarity with her father's usual style ended. This painting was figurative but had a strange other-worldly quality about it. The woman gazing out from the canvas could have been a goddess or a queen.

"Oh Dad!" Grace cried. "Was she really that stunning back then?"

Her father smiled. "To me she was. Even more so probably."

Grace thought of the selkie she had met the night before. In the dark, she had only been able to guess at how she looked. Certainly she hadn't been struck by incredible beauty. Time had changed her, of course, and she had been terribly hurt. But if she had suffered, then she had only got her just deserts. She had ruthlessly seduced Grace's father and then, when the going got tough, abandoned him.

"Dad, I met her," said Grace. "Last night. On the beach. She told me everything."

Her father wasn't shocked.

"I guessed," he said. "I guessed she might turn up. I know she's always around; I just never see her."

Grace gasped. "You know she's around?" she said. "She didn't think you did."

"No...she never really got a grip on how human minds work. Or how devious they can be."

"What do you mean?" asked Grace.

"You said she told you everything."

"Well, she seemed to. I don't really know, of course."

"Did she tell you about the presents?"

"The presents?" A sudden intense excitement gripped Grace. "No – she didn't say anything about any presents."

Grace's dad shook his head. "Hopeless," he said. "She was such an innocent."

"How do you mean, Dad?"

"Every year, the night before your birthday, she comes back. She leaves a little present by your bed. The first time it happened, I couldn't work out where it had come from. Then I noticed the damp patches on the floor. The next year, I could hardly bear it. I lay in wait, desperately wanting to see her. I caught a glimpse through your door and then I knew that I mustn't go in; I mustn't see her again. I knew that if I once had her in my arms again – was even in the same room with her – I couldn't carry on. My carefully built sanity would be shattered. I would follow her to the ends of the earth – and then what would become of you? So I waited, torturing myself, forcing myself to stay downstairs until I thought she had gone. Every year, I've done the same. She doesn't know that I know. And if she did, she'd never expect me to hide the presents from you – so that I wouldn't have to explain."

"You hid the presents? All this time I've thought my mother never thought of me and all the time, you've been hiding her presents?"

"I'm sorry, Grace. I was wrong – just far too selfish. I would rather you lived with the idea of a mother who never thought of you than explain what really happened."

"How could you do that?" said Grace, her voice shaking.

Her father turned away, unable to face her. "Your mother would say exactly the same," he said. "I don't know. It's amazing what depths we can sink to, to protect ourselves. I have no excuse; I can only ask your forgiveness."

Grace walked to the far end of the studio. She couldn't trust herself to speak. She didn't know what she felt any more. Anger, disappointment, shock, pity – it was so confusing she felt physically sick. She took some deep breaths.

"So what about the presents?" she said over her shoulder. "What's happened to them?"

"I've kept them safe for you. I've always meant to tell you eventually. If not before, I would have written a letter before I died and left them with my will.'

"Can I see them now?" said Grace, a catch in her voice. "Please – I want to see them. They are mine, after all."

"Of course. I'll get them out."

Her father turned and went to the cupboard where he kept his paints, a cupboard high on the wall which was always locked and which had always been strictly out of bounds to Grace. Oil paints were expensive, the tools of his trade, and made a terrible mess if spilled; she had needed no other explanation. He took down a large wooden box, just the sort he might keep his materials in.

He placed it on the floor at her feet and, still crouching, looked up into her eyes.

"Can you ever forgive me for hiding this from you?" he said.

Grace wanted to say, "Of course." She wanted the words to trip off her tongue lightly, soothing the guilt that hunched his body. But she couldn't do it. The memory of the dreams – dreams which she now knew were reality – haunted her. She thought of herself, from being a little girl, glimpsing those wonderful presents in the middle of the night, breathing the scent of her mother's fleeting presence, waking each birthday, disappointed to find the presents gone, and her heart was wrung with pity for herself.

"Maybe one day," she forced herself to say. "It's a bit hard just now."

Her father nodded. "I would understand if you never did," he said.

Slowly, hardly daring to breathe, Grace lifted the lid of the box. She knew exactly what she would find there. She couldn't remember much about her early life but the image of every single present was etched on her mind. The first must have been brought when she was three. She lifted it now, a tiny bracelet, strung together from minute pearls, iridescent in the morning sunshine.

"It's probably worth a fortune," said her father, "but I don't expect that matters very much to you at the moment."

"No," said Grace, replacing it carefully and lifting the next, an exquisite little bag, woven from some lustrous sort of seaweed and decorated with glistening discs of mother-of-pearl.

"Do you think she makes them herself?" whispered Grace.

"I don't know," said her father. "She kept the secrets of the selkies very closely guarded. Whether they make these things themselves or whether they trade with merpeople, I don't know."

"Merpeople?" asked Grace, startled.

"Well, of course," said her father. "If selkies exist, then why not merpeople?"

One by one, miracle by miracle, Grace examined her gifts. They were all there, right up to the enchanting necklace she had seen so recently. She gazed at the array before her and for a long time, she couldn't speak.

"I ran away from her," she said, at last. "And all these years she's been watching over me, bringing me presents, sneaking into the house where you were, never forgetting us, just knowing she couldn't live with us. It must have been torture."

"Yes," said her father. "And it's all my—"

Grace suddenly flung her arms round him. "No," she said. "No, don't say it! It's not all your fault. She started it, remember."

"And I should have stopped it. You must go and find her, Grace. Go and show her you understand. Tell her I hid the presents. Tell her whatever you like. But don't let her go away thinking that you hate her."

"But she did leave me, Dad," said Grace. "All the presents in the world can't make up for that. In the end, her own happiness was more important than yours or mine."

"And why shouldn't it be?" said her father, his voice rising angrily. "She had no choice, Grace! Don't you understand? She wouldn't have survived much longer here; she would have gone crazy. And you've been happy enough – don't tell me you haven't! I know everything's suddenly become difficult – but don't pretend you haven't been happy until now!"

Grace nodded. "All right, I've been happy – very happy. But I'm not any more. How can I be? How am I ever going to fit in? How am I going to live a normal life? I'm not normal. I'm covered in fur and I spend half my life in the sea! Nik was getting bored with me – that's another reason he finished with me. He told me to my face I was weird. And that's what everyone thinks really. Jenna and Matt put up with me, of course – they're used to me – but they still think I'm freaky. And now I know why."

Grace's father stood up. "I'm weird too, Grace. Not in the same way as you, of course. But I'm not like a lot of other men; that's why your mother fell in love with me. There's space in the world for weirdos, Grace, you have to believe that. It's not easy – but it's not impossible. Don't give up on happiness, please, Grace. That would break my heart all over again."

Grace began to place her gifts carefully back in their box. "I'll think about it," she said. "Right now, I need some time on my own."

Her father nodded. "Yes," he said. "I think I do too."


Grace carried her box of presents up to her bedroom. Then she laid them all out on her bed. She stroked each one in turn, marvelling at its craftsmanship and beauty. She wanted to tell Matt; he ought to know the reason for all the mad dreams he had listened to. He ought to know that they weren't dreams at all. But she was no longer sure about Matt. Who had been watching her? Just her mother – or Matt as well? What had he been doing on the path last night if he wasn't watching her? But she couldn't ask him. How did you ask probably your closest friend if he'd been stalking you? How insulting was that?

There was only one other person who might know. Her mother. She would have to find her and ask her. Ask her if it was she who disturbed her when she was with Nik on Saturday night, if she had followed her when she was on the beach in the dark, if she had ever seen another watcher. And perhaps Grace could find it in her heart to forgive her and thank her for the presents too. She couldn't escape that last, lonely image of her mother on the beach. It was drawing her down like a magnet.

Grace slipped down the stairs and opened the door of the studio quietly; if her father was working, he didn't like to be disturbed. But he wasn't. He had slumped down on the sofa by the television and was fast asleep. Grace tiptoed across and kissed him lightly on his lined, exhausted face. Then she scribbled a note, propped it up on the kitchen table, changed into her swimsuit, hoodie and joggers and started for the beach.


The bay, as she expected, was empty. It was mid-afternoon and even the local children and their mums, who sometimes found their way down there after school, hadn't arrived yet. Maybe they wouldn't today. The sky was beginning to cloud over; perhaps the heatwave was beginning to break. Grace pulled off her hoodie and joggers and plunged into the waves, enjoying their rise and fall as she swam out into the bay. The sea had been calm for so long that it was refreshing to feel its slight swell.

Grace struck out strongly for the headland and was surprised by how stiff and tired she still felt. Her experiences last night had really taken it out of her. By the time she was halfway there, she was also feeling hungry. She'd breakfasted late and eaten lots of chocolate but had forgotten lunch in the excitement of discovering her gifts. She would have to be careful. If she couldn't find her mother on the rocks with the other seals, she would head straight back. Her search would have to wait for another day.

As she approached the headland, some of the seals flopped into the water, swimming closer as if to check who she was and then backing away again. Grace scanned them for the one she assumed was her mother but she wasn't in the water. Despite what she'd said to Nik, Grace was wary of getting much closer to the seals' home. How would they react if she scrambled up onto the rocks and started a systematic search? Seals weren't aggressive but she knew they had sharp, pointed teeth for fishing which could certainly do her some damage. She trod water, hopefully scanning the colony, all the time horribly aware of how heavy her legs and arms were beginning to feel.

She was just about to give up and start the swim back when she heard her name called. Startled, she turned. Round the corner of the headland, swimming with a grace and strength which she recognized as her own, came a woman, her long hair trailing in the water, just as her own did when she was swimming for pleasure.

"Quickly," called the woman, in her husky voice. "Come with me. The others will keep watch for us."

Grace followed the selkie round the end of the headland. She found her perched on a flat rock, huddled in her cloak which Grace now saw was thick and green and made of a matted material that she couldn't place.

"Felted seaweed," said the selkie, noting her curious gaze.

They sat in silence for a while. Grace couldn't find the words to begin. In the dull light of an ordinary summer afternoon, it seemed bizarre to be sitting on the end of a headland, surrounded by seals, with a naked woman wrapped in a cloak of seaweed. To address her as her mother seemed completely impossible.

"So why have you come, Grace?" the selkie asked at last. "I thought you hated your mother and never wanted to see her again? That's the impression she got, anyway."

With a shock of alarm, Grace looked more closely at the selkie. Her face was deeply lined and her hair, on closer inspection, was streaked with white.

"Who are you?" Grace gasped. "I thought you *were* my mother."

The selkie shook her head. "She's gone, Grace. I don't know if she'll come back. She didn't want to stay where she wasn't welcome."

"I didn't know everything then!" gasped Grace, her heart pounding. "I didn't understand how awful it must have been for her!"

"And you do now?"

"Dad told me. He said she would have gone mad if she'd stayed. I know what he means; I nearly went crazy myself when I had the flu and couldn't swim. He blames himself completely."

"Poor Robert. Of course it wasn't all his fault. She played her part, the silly girl, despite all my warnings. She knew the stories but she was always wayward, right from being a little one."

Grace stared into the selkie's eyes and saw her own staring back.

"I know who you are!" she exclaimed. "You're my grandmother!"

The selkie nodded. "Yes. And now I, like many a grandmother before me, am left to sort out the mess my daughter has made."

"She didn't mean to make a mess," rejoined Grace, firing up. "She never meant to hurt anyone."

"No – but she has, hasn't she? You said you never wanted to see her again. You must have had a reason."

"It was because of my dad. And because she left me. And...because of my skin.

"Your skin? What do you mean?"

For reply, Grace held out an arm. "Feel it," she said.

Grace's grandmother reached out a wondering finger and ran it down Grace's arm.

"It covers you entirely?" she said, at last.

Grace nodded.

"I'm sorry," said the grandmother, her voice pained. "I've never heard of this happening to a selkie child. Strange fingernails, no ears, whiskers – I've heard of all those – but not this. When you were born, your mother was so thrilled. You looked just like any other human child; she had been so terrified that you would be half-seal – and then, of course, you would have died."

A thrill of horror ran through Grace. She had never considered that possibility. To be half-seal – and to die!

"I was lucky then," she said. "Well, sort of."

"I'm glad you think so," said her grandmother, "but I can see that life will be hard for you."

Grace nodded again. "It isn't easy. I keep telling myself people have to put up with worse things but it doesn't help much."

For a while they were both quiet.

"So what will you do now?" asked the old selkie. "Go home and try to pretend this never happened? That you never met your mother."

Grace jumped slightly. "No, I have to go now. I have to find her. There's something I have to tell her. And something I have to ask."

Her grandmother shrugged. "She may have gone to the beach where she first met Robert; she often goes there in her bleakest hours."

"Where is it?" demanded Grace.

"Not far – a little way along the coast. It's a tiny cove – you can only reach it from the sea. Your father had rowed there, the day they met."

"I know it!" said Grace. "We've been to it for picnics! It's an easy enough swim from here."

"Well, if you really must find her, then go. If she isn't there, I have no idea."

Grace didn't stop to think any further. "Goodbye,

grandmother," she said. "And thank you. Will we meet again?"

"That entirely depends on you, Grace," said her grandmother. "We are always here, as you know."

Grace smiled at the dignified, stern old selkie. "Then I'm sure we will," she said and dived into the water.

# 13

Matt hurried up the road from the bus stop, hunching against the stiff breeze that had sprung out of the dull, sultry afternoon. He paused by his own house to watch the gnarled, salt-blasted tree in the garden appear to lift its branches and shake them, reaching up like a great bird about to take off. He loved these moments at the start of a storm when the trees and the buildings seemed to enjoy a few moments of a different life. He relished the force of the wind in his hair and its blast against his sweaty body.

Then he hurried on to Grace's house.

When she hadn't appeared for school, he had guessed that she was exhausted from her stupid swim of the night before; he wanted to check that she was all right now.

The kitchen door was open as usual.

"Grace!" he called, as he entered. "It's me, Matt."

She wasn't in the kitchen. He didn't like to go upstairs without permission so he knocked on the studio door. No answer. He tried again.

Robert's voice answered groggily. "Is that you, Grace? You can come in."

"No, it's Matt, Mr. Hornby," said Matt. "I was looking for Grace."

Robert opened the door. He was dishevelled from his long sleep. "Have you tried her room?" he said, rubbing his eyes.

"Grace!" Matt shouted and then ran up the stairs. "She isn't here, Mr. Hornby," he called down.

Robert and Matt looked at each other.

"Has she gone for a swim?" asked Matt.

"She might have done," said Robert. "She might have gone...looking for someone. Oh Matt – it's a long story."

"Mr. Hornby, that doesn't matter. Look at the weather."

The studio's windows gave them an ample view. Outside, the light had faded. Dark storm clouds had massed over Thurle Bay and the sea beneath was a sinister grey, lashed with spume-flecked waves. As they watched, the first rush of rain came pelting down.

"She's a very strong swimmer," said Robert, his voice faint.

"Not that strong," said Matt.


By the time Grace reached the cove, the sky was darkening. She couldn't see anyone on the beach but explored it anyway. No one was there. She knew it well from visits with her father. There were no caves or other hiding places. Grace felt chilled with disappointment. If her mother wasn't here, where could she be? Had she swum away for ever? Would Grace never see her again?

Looking at the sky, however, Grace realized that she had other problems. A strong breeze had sprung up and already the sea was looking angry. There was no way up the cliffs that surrounded the cove and she knew that, once the tide turned, the sandy beach would be covered. If she stayed, she would be beaten against the cliffs by the mounting waves. Her only way home was to swim back the way she had come – and quickly.

For the first time ever, she entered the sea with dread in her heart. She knew she was too tired and hungry for this swim if the conditions worsened. Her only hope was that the storm would build slowly and she could get back before her energy ran out.

She struck out firmly but not overfast; she needed to go swiftly but not to burn herself out. Already the waves were troubling her; the tide was on the turn. If she didn't find the strength to fight it, she would simply be swept back onto the rocky shore.

*Don't panic,* Grace told herself. *You cannot afford to panic.*

She was glad now of all her school swimming: the disciplined training to pace herself over long races, the control of her breathing to remain calm and effective. She needed all her experience now. The waves were rising around her, already almost a metre high, so that she felt she was making little progress – and she knew they could get far, far higher. She started to dive beneath them, hoping that would be quicker and easier, but it made little difference. When she emerged it took valuable time for her to get her bearings. The sky was darkening rapidly and Grace could hardly see her only landmark, the headland of Thurle Bay, even when it wasn't obscured by waves.

She had been swimming for about twenty minutes when the rain began, pelting down in a torrent which almost suffocated her. She stopped swimming and trod water frantically, mouthing for air. Panic threatened to engulf her. Between the rain and the waves, she could see virtually nothing. Even if she carried on swimming, she had no guarantee she would be going in the right direction. Against the tide, she might even be making no progress at all. Would she be best to press on or to conserve her energy, trying to ride the waves and praying that she could outlast the storm? Her dad might call the coastguard, of course, and the lifeboat might be launched. She was sure he would guess she was in the sea.

The thought of her father's terror and the danger that would threaten the lifeboat crew fired her adrenalin. She couldn't give up out here; she simply had to get back. Matt's father was a lifeboatman and so was Mr. Thomson, her PE teacher; she couldn't bear to put them at risk. And she absolutely must not die; what would become of her father then? She tried to swim calmly, firmly, not pushing herself too hard but holding her own against the strength of the tide.

The theory was good but the desperate feeling of heaviness in her body and the lethargy that was creeping into her brain were, she knew, quite deadly.

\* \* \*

The sleepy fug in Robert's head cleared the moment he realized Grace might be in the sea. He leaped for the studio door and in seconds had Grace's note in his hand.

"She's gone to the bay," he said, his face ashen.

Matt swore.

"We mustn't panic," said Robert. "She may be back any moment. If she was only swimming in the bay, she should have seen the storm coming and got ashore in time."

"What are we waiting for?" said Matt. "Let's go and look! I've got my mobile. If we can't find her, we'll call the coastguard."

"Ring your mother," said Robert. "Tell her where you are. I'll find you some waterproofs."

A few minutes later, Robert and Matt were hurrying down the path to the bay. Robert had quickly packed a hot Thermos, flashlight and dry clothes for Grace.

"Shouldn't we take a rope?" asked Matt, battling to make himself heard over the wind and the rain.

"There's rope in my boat and a lifebelt and line on the beach," said Robert.

"What about flares? If she's in the water, she may not be able to see which way to swim."

"In the boat!" shouted Robert. "I always keep a few there."

At every treacherous footstep into the gloom, they hoped to spot Grace struggling up the path to meet them.

It was a fight to stay upright in the wind, with the muddy shingle slipping away beneath their feet.

"At least the wind's onshore!" bellowed Matt. "It'll bring her in. And the tide has turned too."

Robert didn't want to discourage him. Fine, if Grace was safely in the middle of the bay: if she wasn't, an onshore wind and incoming tide would simply dash her against the rocks.

They reached the bay. It was as dark as a wintry afternoon but they could still see that no one was on the beach. Waves rearing a couple of metres high were crashing down onto the rocks that lay at the far edge of the sand. Even someone who knew the beach as well as Grace did would have difficulty in finding the gap.

Both Robert and Matt had seen far worse conditions but that was no comfort. This was bad enough. If Grace was out there in the bay, neither of them could see any way that she could get back alive.

"Should we launch your boat?" shouted Matt in desperation.

"Are you mad? We'd never get it off the sand," Robert answered. "I'll light a flare. You ring the coastguard."

"But we don't know where she is!" hollered Matt.

"I'll do it," Robert snatched the phone. "I think I can guess where she's gone. You light the flare."

* * *

Grace was beginning to flounder; it was becoming too much effort to ride with the waves, let alone make any progress home.

*If I can just make it to the headland,* she told herself, *I can sit out the storm. It's not winter; I won't die of exposure – and the selkies would help me, I'm sure.*

But she couldn't even see the headland. She was lost in a raging sea with no means of telling which way to swim.

She was crying now, although her face was so wet and so often underwater that she only knew because of the heaving of her chest.

*How stupid,* she told herself, *wasting energy on crying.* But the thought of her dad without her, and of her mum not knowing that she understood and forgave her, was too much to bear. She would die crying for their grief; she couldn't help it. *Perhaps I won't die,* she thought. *Perhaps the Daughters of the Air will take pity on me and I will become one of them for ever.* And then she realized that was the end of *The Little Mermaid's* story, not her own.

She had done as much as she could; there seemed to be no energy left in her body, no will in her heart. She simply wanted to slip away into the water and sleep.

There was nothing to see anyway so Grace closed her eyes. The sea was her real home; she would rest there.

"Well?" Matt shouted. "Are they sending the lifeboat out?"

"It's going to be tough. Onshore wind and the tide coming in. They'll have difficulty getting out but they'll go."

Matt nodded. He knew the scenario. His dad had been there many times before. When they got Grace back (he couldn't consider for a second the possibility that they wouldn't) she would hate herself for causing them to go.

"What now?" he shouted.

"More flares," yelled Robert. "There's still a chance that she's in the bay."

Matt wanted to send up flares continuously; it was something to do. But they only had a few and Robert was cautious.

"If she sees one and makes for it, she'll need another one a few minutes later to guide her in," he insisted. "We have to be patient."

Matt didn't know how Robert could stand it; he felt as if he was going crazy himself. He wanted to stand at the edge of the sea and scream Grace's name into the wind or fling himself into the waves to find her –

anything rather than wait, battered by the storm, with hope dying by the minute.

Suddenly, another figure appeared out of the gloom beside them. Relief sprang for a second in Matt's heart and vanished instantly.

"Jenna!" he said. "What are you doing here?"

"Your mum rang to tell us," Jenna told him, struggling to make herself heard. "Your dad's been called out to crew the lifeboat. I've brought more flares."

"You star!" said Matt, giving her a quick hug. "Mr. Hornby, did you hear that?"

"Great!" shouted Robert. "Let's get another one up then."


Grace was dreaming again. The smell of the ocean was strong in her nostrils and the window had juddered off its latch and was banging in the sea breeze. Beneath her, the bed seemed to be rocking from side to side. *Bobbing along, bobbing along on the bottom of the beautiful briny sea,* ran a persistent little tune in her head. Her bed was definitely on some sort of journey. And then, loud in her ear, she heard a fierce barking unlike any dog's she had ever met. A cold, wet nose was thrust into her face and she could feel the tickle of whiskers.

She came round with a jolt. Nuzzling her persistently in the face was a seal.

"Mother?" Grace whispered and, from some reserve of energy she didn't know she had, managed to wrap her leaden arms around the seal's neck. It barked urgently, rolling its body under hers so that she was draped across its back. Then it began to swim. Somehow Grace's brain jolted back into action; she understood what was needed. She couldn't be a deadweight for her mother to carry. Clinging on with her arms, she kicked out with her legs, even though they felt as if they had lead boots attached. Looking up, she saw something bright shooting up into the sky. A flare! And not far away either. Her mother was heading towards it. Perhaps...and Grace could hardly bear to hope...perhaps she had managed to swim further than she had thought. Perhaps someone, her dad maybe, was sending up flares from the beach for her to see.

In a sudden lull in the noise of the wind, Matt heard his mobile ringing. He rummaged inside his waterproofs and dragged it out.

"Mum?" he said. "What's going on? Oh, right, I see. Oh, okay. We'll stay here then. Okay. Bye."

"What is it?" Robert looked up from his next flare.

"Mum's down at the lifeboat station," he said. "They're about to put out but it doesn't look too good. They're going to make slow progress."

Robert nodded. "Best just carry on here, then," he said. "There's nothing else we can do."

Jenna had been standing, staring out to sea, her eyes straining for the slightest sign of anything that might be Grace. Suddenly, she grabbed Matt's arm.

"Look!" she shrieked. "Out there! I saw something, I'm certain I did!"

Matt followed the line of her pointing arm. She was right, he was sure. There was something there, something darker than the waves, something more solid.

"Send that one up, Mr. Hornby!" he shouted and reached for the flashlight.

Together, Matt and Jenna ran down the beach, the flashlight illuminating their path. Matt could see the shape clearly now. It kept rising on the waves and falling again, a rounded, blob-like shape, not quite human – but it had to be Grace, it simply had to be.


Several times, Grace nearly lost her grip. There was nothing to cling onto so she could only lock her fingers round her mother's neck. The combined effects of exhaustion and cold meant there was barely any feeling in her hands. She only knew her fingers had unlocked when she found herself slipping down the seal's body. Now, approaching the shore with the waves mounting to breakpoint, it was even more difficult to keep her grip. Her brain was so numbed that all she could do was summon the last dregs of her energy to hang on.

Another flare, much closer now. They were approaching the shelf of rock that guarded the beach. Grace was too tired to be terrified. Her mother knew the bay even better than she did; she trusted her to find the gap.

They were riding the swell now, like a bodyboard and its rider, but there had to come a moment when they fell from the wave's crest or dived down into it; if not, they would overshoot the gap in the rocks.

Grace's mother gave a bark of warning and the next moment dived down the steep wall of the breaking wave. Her body thrust violently forward, clearly trying to get as far in as possible before the wave came crashing down on them. All was froth and darkness and confusion for Grace as she clung on with the very last of her strength. Her lungs were bursting for air; she was convinced she was dying. She was aware of a bright light glowing ahead of her.

*This is what people talk about – the light that you follow when you're near to death,* she thought vaguely. She didn't feel sad any more, just relieved; she was nearly there now. Soon she would be able to rest for ever.

"Whatever it is, it's coming in!" shouted Jenna.

Robert was already running down the beach; he too could see the dark shape in the water.

"Hold the light steady, Matt!" he yelled. "It'll guide her in!"

"Oh no, look at that wave!" cried Matt.

They watched in horror as Grace and her mother rose over two metres in the air, before they disappeared down the wave wall.

"Where's she gone?" bellowed Robert. "Can you pick her out, Matt?"

"She must be trying to find the gap," shouted Matt. "But I can't see her!"

Jenna came stumbling down the beach, struggling with the lifebelt and line. "Shall we throw this out? She might be able to grab it!"

For reply, Matt grabbed the lifebelt and wriggled into it.

"Hang on to the line," he shouted. "I'm going in!"

"Matt, no!" yelled Robert. "It's too dangerous."

"Try and stop me," bellowed Matt. "Just hold that light so I can see!" Then he waded into the sea, groping in the darkness for whatever the dark shape had been.

In the dream, something or someone was hauling Grace out of bed. Bright light hurt her eyes. It must be morning but she was too tired to get up and go to school. She just wanted to be left to sleep for ever and ever.

"No, no," she moaned. "Leave me alone."

"She said something – she's still breathing," said Robert, helping Matt to drag Grace clear of the waves. "Quick, turn her over!"

All three of them knew what to do with someone who had nearly drowned. Within moments, they had Grace coughing and spluttering and retching up sea water.

"Ring the coastguard," said Robert. "The lifeboat can go back in but we need medical help."

Jenna had run for the clothes and blanket for Grace. Together they wrapped her up and huddled round her to keep her warm. In the beam of the flashlight, her face was grey and ghostly.

"Mother," she gasped. "Where's Mother?"

"What did she say?" demanded Jenna.

"She's raving," said Robert, who was close enough to hear her words.

"No, Mr. Hornby, she's not," said Matt. "There was a seal in the water too. I saw it. I'm sorry, Mr. Hornby – there was blood in the water. It must have hurt itself on the rocks."

Robert's eyes met Matt's, startled.

"It's okay, I know," said Matt. "I'll explain later."

"Right," said Robert, nodding slowly. "So where's the seal now?"

"I don't know. I only saw it for a moment."

Robert took the flashlight and ran down to the water's edge.

"What's he doing? What were you on about? Is he looking for a hurt seal?" demanded Jenna.

"It's a long story," Matt said. "Don't worry."

Robert ran back up the beach. "I can't see anything," he said, "but I don't like to leave Grace."

Matt gripped his arm. "I expect the seal swam away," he said. "Best leave it, Mr. Hornby."

Robert nodded but his eyes were wild.

"At least we have Grace back," said Matt.

"Yes," said Robert. "At least we have Grace."

# 14

Grace was lucky. It was a long way to the hospital so a doctor came out to the cottage to check her over, the one she had seen about her fur. He felt it was safe simply to let her sleep and promised to visit the next day.

"You're in remarkably good shape, considering," he said when he examined her the next morning. "I hear you're a champion swimmer. You're obviously extremely fit."

"Thank you," said Grace, managing a wan smile. She didn't feel remotely fit. It had been almost more than she could manage to stagger from her bed to the loo, even with her dad to support her.

The doctor looked down at her, hesitating.

"You know," he said, "that problem you consulted me about – the one I referred to the specialists..."

"You mean my fur," said Grace, with a wry smile.

"Yes. I know it's a very distressing problem – but it occurs to me that it could have saved your life. You were in the sea a very long time. I would have expected hypothermia to set in. It seems to me that, in effect, you had your own built-in wetsuit. It would have trapped some air and insulated you. I assume that's why seals are furry."

A curious look crossed Grace's face.

"Of course!" she said. "Thank you so much for saying that. I never thought of it that way."

"I'm glad if it helps," said the doctor, visibly relaxing. "You'll get a letter about appointments with the specialists before long, I hope, but I just thought you may want to reconsider...maybe it actually helps with your swimming? Streamlining or something?"

"I'll think about it," said Grace. "I've got a lot to think about just now. But thank you. Thank you very much."

\* \* \*

Matt was her next visitor.

"Shouldn't you be at school?" asked Grace.

"I'm skiving," he grinned. "I reckoned major trauma was a reasonable excuse."

"Major trauma?"

"Watching your best friend nearly drown," said Matt. "Don't you think that's traumatic enough?"

Grace smiled. "What about Jenna?"

"Oh, she's gone to school. Can't wait to tell everyone all about it. You know Jenna. I'm sure she'll be along later."

There was an awkward silence, broken by both of them at once.

"Grace, I..."

"Matt..."

They laughed. "You first," said Matt.

Grace found herself blushing. "I don't know how to explain this, Matt," she said, "but I'd begun to think you were...well, stalking me, actually."

Matt sat back, looking stunned. Then his expression changed. "Of course – the watcher! You thought it was me!"

"It seemed to fit. You were so peculiar when I started going out with Nik – and then, the other night when I met you on the path – what on earth were you doing there?

You never explained. And your hair – and the baggy clothes you wear. They seemed to fit the person I thought I saw. I know who it was now but...well...I'm still worried. What *were* you doing on the path that night?"

It was Matt's turn to blush and with his fair colouring, he went scarlet.

"I wasn't watching *you*," he blurted out. "I was watching your mother."

"My mother? But...how did you know about her?"

Matt sighed. "It's a long story. I first saw her one day on the beach years ago. I was running down to meet you. You were playing in the sand with your dad. She was hiding and she didn't see me. At first I thought she was just a normal person, changing behind a rock under a big towel. Then I realized she was watching you. There was no one else on the beach. I was going to tell your dad but I was so busy watching her that I tripped up and fell. When I got up, she'd gone. I was really spooked, I can tell you, but I reckoned I must have imagined it. Some of the big boulders are awfully funny shapes."

"But you saw her again?"

"Yes. And you started telling me about your dreams. I didn't see her very often; sometimes I'd think I'd imagined her. But then I'd see her again. She never seemed to see me; maybe her eyesight isn't too good or maybe she was so focused on you that she just blanked me out. Then I started noticing that the seals hang around when you're swimming. Generally, they keep away when there are people in the water. I remembered an old story from a picture book I had when I was little. It was so sad – about a selkie whose skin was stolen by a man who wanted her to be his wife – d'you know the one? It seemed crazy at first but the more I thought about it, the more it seemed to fit what had happened to you – except that I couldn't imagine your dad doing something so rotten. For years, I kept telling myself it couldn't be true – there must be some other explanation. Then I discovered how bad I felt when Nik asked you out. I wanted to throttle him. Anything's possible, I realized, when you're in love – even stealing a selkie's skin."

"In love?" said Grace, her voice amazed.

"Yes, Grace, in love. You're so naïve, you know. Jenna's suspected for ages – she's always been a bit jealous of our friendship – but you seemed completely blind."

"But why didn't you say anything?"

Matt shrugged. "What was the point? You never seemed to notice me like that; in fact, you didn't seem to notice boys at all – until Nik hit on you. Anyway, it made me think about your dad. I reckoned that even a kind, gentle man like him might feel desperate – willing to do whatever it took."

"But *you* didn't do anything," said Grace.

"No, but I wanted to. Instead, I started watching your mother watching you. I convinced myself that she was waiting to take her revenge on your dad. She'd left him, hadn't she? She must hate him for what he'd done. So what might she steal from him?"

"Me?" said Grace, wide-eyed.

"That's what I was afraid of – that she might be going to lure you away somehow. It was a good excuse to keep tabs on you – and Nik, of course. I was there on Saturday when she disturbed you and Nik. And on Monday evening, I rang a couple of times and you didn't answer, so I started out for the beach. That's why I was on the path. I could persuade myself I was the hero, waiting to rescue you. It was rubbish, obviously."

"But you did, Matt. You did rescue me. Dad told me how you waded into the sea on the end of the line and dragged me out. He said there was no stopping you."

Matt shook his head. "It was your mother that saved your life, Grace, not me. Who knows how far she swam with you? I only dragged you out of the shallows. I was mad to think she might take you away – even if she could. Your mum brought you home, Grace – you never needed a minder. She was just worried because you'd started going out with boys. All mothers are. It's obvious now — especially when you think about what happened to her."

Silent tears were running down Grace's face. "All that time, I thought she didn't care," said Grace. "It must have been hell for her. And now she's hurt – she may be dead!"

"How long have you known the truth?"

"Only since the day before yesterday. I met her on the beach."

"I thought your dad must have told you about your mum," said Matt. "When you said there was something strange about you..."

"I just meant my fur."

Matt nodded. "When you had that shower it was a shock – but I was kind of expecting it. That's when I really knew. It all finally fitted together."

Grace wiped her face on her sleeve.

"Last night, I went to look for her – on the beach where she first met Dad. That's why I was out there when the storm came up. I wanted to tell her that I understood. That I didn't mean all the dreadful things I'd said to her the night before, how I hated her for leaving us and breaking Dad's heart. I didn't know the full story then. I couldn't find her, though, and now it might be too late."

"She wasn't dead when I saw her bring you in," said Matt. "Only hurt."

"Hurt and bleeding in that dreadful sea? I don't want to think about it. Dad's gone to look for her again – I just hope he doesn't find something awful."

Dumbly, Matt shifted up the bed towards her and held out his arms. Grace collapsed into them. "Oh Matt," she sobbed. "I don't think I can bear it."

Robert Hornby returned about ten minutes later and was startled to walk in to find Matt kissing his daughter's tear-stained face. He cleared his throat.

"She isn't on the beach," he said.

Grace shrank back under the covers.

"Well...um...that's a good sign then," said Matt, blushing.

Robert shook his head.

"I rowed out to the headland," he told them.

"And?" said Grace.

"The seal colony has gone," said Robert.

Matt saw grief hit Grace like a mallet. Quietly, he left. Right then, the only person she needed was her dad.

\* \* \*

Grace sat up with a soft cry. Something had woken her, she didn't know what. A sudden chill, a flutter on the air, the sound of a light footfall – it could have been any of these. She glanced around the room, lit up by bright moonlight. There was no one there but the night smelled of the sea.

Hardly daring to breathe, Grace peered at her bedside table. The letter she had written in a feverish moment of hope and left propped up against her photo of Matt, had gone. In its place, shimmering in the soft light of the moon, was a simple ring of mother-of-pearl. As Grace slipped it onto her finger, its cool, immaculate smoothness spoke of years and years in the sea. Grace sat up in her bed, hugging her hand to her heart, tears filling her eyes as a huge, year-long boulder of pain melted in her chest. She would wear this ring for ever, just as she wore her fur. It was part of her story.

She knew that she should tell her father at once, that this was news that simply couldn't wait until the morning, but for a few minutes, she sat, savouring the knowledge for herself. Then she threw back the quilt and ran through to her father.

She looked down at him. His hair was more sparse than it had been a year ago and his face more lined. She rested her hand on his shoulder and shook him gently, but it was the tear that landed on his cheek that woke him.

"Gracie?" he murmured. "Grace? What's the matter?"

For answer, she held out her hand with its ring. "Look, Daddy," she said. "Look what she's left for my birthday. She didn't die that night. She's alive."

If you loved Fur, you might also
enjoy these other captivating reads.

# Mirror, Mirror
## Nancy Butcher

When Princess Ana discovers that her mother
has something to do with the sinister illness sweeping
through the Academy, she realizes she must confront the
truth to save her friends.

A lyrical and timeless story of beauty to die for.

0 7460 7309 7

# Flying South
## L.M. Elliott

Storm clouds are gathering for Alice with the arrival of
her mother's new boyfriend. Will an unlikely friendship
give her the power to protect those she loves?

A warm and tender coming-of-age story, set against the
tumultuous backdrop of the 1960s American Deep South.

0 7460 7381 X

# Yankee Girl
## Mary Ann Rodman

Alice is torn between standing up for the only black girl
in her school, and being popular with the in-crowd.
When tragedy strikes will she find the courage to act?

A poignant story about racism and doing the right thing.

0 7460 6749 6